The Luckie Star

by Ann Waldron

E. P. Dutton | New York

Library of Congress Cataloging in Publication Data

Waldron, Ann   The Luckie star

SUMMARY: A twelve-year-old is not anticipating the
family's summer in Florida but involvement with sunken
treasure and her family's recognition of her as an
anomaly make the whole thing worthwhile.

[1. Florida—Fiction.   2. Buried treasure—Fiction]
I. Title.
PZ7.W1465Lu   [Fic]   76-30371   ISBN 0-525-34270-2

Published simultaneously in Canada by Clarke,
Irwin & Company Limited, Toronto and Vancouver

Editor: Ann Durell   Designer: Riki Levinson

Printed in the U.S.A.   First Edition
10 9 8 7 6 5 4 3 2 1

The Luckie Star

For Booj

Acknowledgments

I should like to thank Clifton and George Lewis II for advising me about sailing off the North Florida coast.

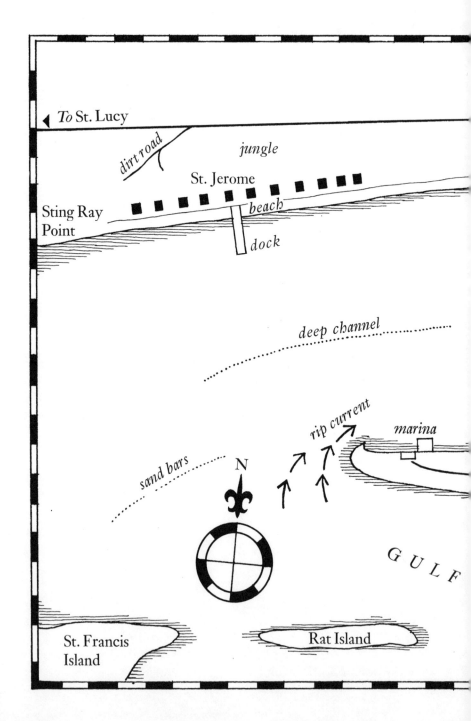

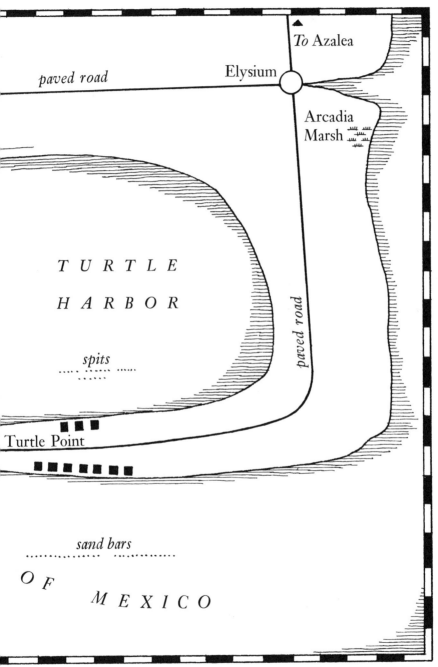

To Azalea

paved road

Elysium

Arcadia
Marsh

TURTLE

HARBOR

spits

Turtle Point

sand bars

OF

MEXICO

paved road

Map by Richard Cuffari

One

How do you smuggle a telescope into the family station wagon for a thousand-mile trip to Florida?

You don't, Quincy Luckie finally decided. You have to brazen it out. She carefully packed her telescope into its original box, which was three feet long, one foot wide, and one foot deep, and placed the box at the top of the stairs along with all the other things that were going to the beach with them.

There was Melissa's paint box and Sam's camera bag. There were three guitars; two cartons of books, both of them overflowing; her mother's typewriter, her father's typewriter, Melissa's typewriter; and her mother's needle-point basket.

The telescope looked very small in the midst of all that, Quincy decided. Maybe nobody would notice it at all. She went downstairs to see if supper was ready.

It wasn't. Her father was in the kitchen chopping fruit for fruit salad. Quincy started toward the stove to see what was in the pot simmering gently on the stove.

"Dammit!" said her father, "get away from that stove!"

1

"Where's Mama?" Quincy asked.

"She'll be here soon," Mr. Luckie said.

When Mrs. Luckie got home from her job teaching acting to children at the Alley Theater, all the Luckies—Mr. Luckie, Mrs. Luckie, Melissa, Jill, Sam, and Quincy—sat down, and Mr. Luckie began to serve the plates from the head of the table.

"Thank heavens," said Mrs. Luckie, "we'll be at St. Jerome in a week. And we'll have the whole summer!"

"Swimming," said Melissa, who was eighteen.

"Sailing," said Sam, who was fourteen.

"The Summer Show," said Jill, who was sixteen.

"You know," said Quincy, who was twelve, "I'd just as soon stay here one summer."

"Stay here one summer? What do you mean?"

"Not go to St. Jerome?"

"Stay here in Houston?"

"Crazy Ducky!"

"What's the matter with you, Ducky?" her father said. "I thought everybody in this house couldn't wait to get over to North Florida and sit around all summer."

"I like to go to St. Jerome all right," Quincy said. "I would just like to not go every single summer."

"You mean you'd rather stay here, *here* in Houston, than go to the beach?" Jill asked her.

"Isn't Ducky a funny little baby?" said Melissa. Melissa had just graduated from high school and had been accepted at Bennington College and she was very, very adult all of a sudden. Quincy hated her.

"You mean you really don't want to go to the beach, Ducky?" Mrs. Luckie said. "You don't want to go see Grandmama and Grandpapa and go scalloping and go sail-

2

ing and get tanned and help with the Summer Show?"

"Just one summer I'd like to be close to a library and I'd like to go to the summer school for high school students at Rice and take computer programming and astronomy. . . ."

"Computer programming!"

"Astronomy!"

"Library! But we take lots of books with us."

"You're sick!"

"Poor baby!"

What a family, thought Quincy, as they all rattled on. Then they began to talk about the trip. They were her own family, Quincy thought, but they would never, never understand as long as they lived that somebody might be interested in something like science or mathematics. All they could understand was books and stories and plays and art and music—and the beach.

"Dammit! Can't I even get started on my own dinner before you send your plate for seconds?" her father was saying to Sam, who had managed to clean up his plate during the discussion and was holding it out toward his father for seconds.

Sam put his plate down. "I can wait," he said.

"That's all right, Oliver Twist," said Mr. Luckie. "I was just kidding. Pass it on down."

Sam passed it.

Nobody noticed the telescope until the day before they left for the beach.

"Dammit! What's this thing?"

Quincy was downstairs when she heard her father yelling upstairs. She hesitated. She *knew* he was talking about

3

the telescope. She stood on one foot hesitating. Maybe it would all blow over.

"Sarah!" her father called her mother. "Sarah! We've got too much stuff laid out here to go to the beach. We'll never get it all in the station wagon. Or if we do, *we* can't go. Maybe that's the best plan—just drive the car down and leave the family here."

"Honey, we can put a lot of stuff on top," Mrs. Luckie said in a soothing voice.

"Not if we're going to go under the underpasses on Interstate 10," said Mr. Luckie. "And don't use that soothing tone to me."

"We've always managed before," Mrs. Luckie said. "You're very clever at packing the car."

Mr. Luckie was not mollified by flattery.

"What IS this thing?" he said.

"It's a telescope," her mother said. "Isn't it?"

"Who's taking a telescope?" her father said.

"I don't know," her mother said.

"I am." Quincy decided to face the music, and she started up the stairs. "I put the telescope there. I want to take it with me."

"What for?"

"I want to look at the planets," Quincy said. What idiots they were sometimes, she thought. "The stars," she explained, as her mother looked bewildered.

Her father's attention seemed to wander off to another problem.

"Look at all these books!" he said. "We can't take all these books."

"You put a lot of them out here yourself," Mrs. Luckie said. "All those texts of morality plays and miracle plays are yours."

"My God, we'll never get down there," Mr. Luckie said.

"Yes, we will." Mrs. Luckie stayed calm.

"Well, we can't take that needlepoint and we can't take that telescope," Mr. Luckie said.

"I'll hold my needlepoint basket in my lap," said Mrs. Luckie.

"I'll hold my telescope in my lap," said Quincy.

"You can't hold that three-foot carton in your lap all the way to Florida," said Mr. Luckie.

"I should say not," said Melissa, entering the fray. "You'd stick it into everybody."

"Who asked you?" said Quincy. "I'll sit in the very back of the wagon and hold it."

"You can't sit back there," her father said. "It's going to be packed with our clothes and our sheets and towels and the few little things your mother can't leave the house without. . . ."

"Oh, for heaven's sake," Mrs. Luckie said. "I know it will all go in. It always does."

"We never took a telescope before, and we never took two cartons of books before. . . ."

"We *always* take two cartons of books," Mrs. Luckie said.

"I know the car will drag the concrete on the highways," Mr. Luckie said. He began carrying cartons down the stairs to load the car.

Jill came out of her room. "Is it safe to come out?" she asked. "I hate packing day."

"All quiet," Quincy said. "For now, anyway."

She went to her room, picked up an Arthur C. Clarke book, and left the earth.

Two

The trip to St. Jerome took the next two days and it was, everyone agreed, pure hell. They were very crowded in the station wagon, and everyone blamed the telescope for the terrible discomfort. If it hadn't been for the telescope, they said, there would have been plenty of room. They would have made better time, too, and the trip would have been shorter.

"Why do you want to bring that dumb telescope?" Melissa asked Quincy at one point.

"Why do you want to bring paints and all those guitars?" Quincy asked her.

"That's different," Melissa said.

"We need all the guitars for the Summer Show," Jill said.

"Oh, the Show, the wonderful, stupendous Show," Quincy said.

"Oh, come on, Ducky, you like the Show, too," Jill said.

"Big deal," Quincy said.

Quincy was fighting back, on the defensive about her

telescope, but her heart wasn't in the attack on the Show. She knew how much Jill, especially, enjoyed the Show. And the Show wasn't all bad, she had to admit to herself. The Luckies always produced a Summer Show at the end of the season at St. Jerome. Mr. Luckie was consultant, Mrs. Luckie directed, and everybody helped. Everybody who stayed in St. Jerome was invited, even urged, to take a part in the Show or to help with the staging, and most people did. But the Luckies were responsible.

"It *is* a big deal," Jill said. "But where did you get that telescope?"

"At a garage sale," Quincy said. "That sale where you bought that old sheet music and Mama bought that mirror with the silver coming off."

"How funny," said Jill.

Why was it, Quincy wondered, that it was so funny to buy a telescope at a garage sale but fine and dandy for Jill to buy music and her mother to buy junk? If you found a telescope at a garage sale for five dollars, nobody in this family would realize what a bargain you'd found. They thought you were an idiot.

Quincy loved her telescope. The sky in Houston had been too hazy with pollution to see much, and she was looking forward to the clear skies of St. Jerome. She'd brought along a book she'd bought with her own money, a book on stargazing, and it told you how to use a telescope and how to find the planets and the constellations. With a telescope even smaller than hers, you could see Saturn's rings and four moons of Jupiter, according to the book.

The phrases "Saturn's rings" and "moons of Jupiter" made Quincy tingle. She knew they were there, up in the sky, but if she could see them for herself, it would be well worth all the fuss about bringing the telescope.

7

She shut her ears to the rest of the family and read the section on Jupiter in the book again.

Finally, in the middle of the afternoon of the second day, they got to St. Jerome. They turned off the paved state road and drove down a rutted sandy track through palmetto scrub and thickets of yaupon, which the Luckie children had always called the Jungle, and came out into a clearing behind the houses that made up the summer colony of St. Jerome.

They pulled into the driveway to their house, which, like all the houses, faced the water of Turtle Harbor.

The young people tumbled out, and their parents got out more slowly.

"Isn't it heavenly?" Quincy heard her mother say, as she walked with the others toward the water.

"There's Grandmama!" said Sam.

"And Grandpapa," said Jill.

Mr. and Mrs. Ballew were hurrying down the path that connected their yard with the Luckies' yard, and they all met between the two houses.

Grandpapa had his pipe in his mouth and wore the same old floppy-brimmed fishing hat that he'd worn every summer they could remember. And Grandmama had her knitting bag over one arm.

There was much exclaiming about how well everyone looked . . . how big and strong the grandchildren looked and how young and healthy the grandparents looked, with Mr. and Mrs. Luckie smiling distractedly at both the other generations.

And there was much attention for Melissa—to Quincy's rage—because she'd just graduated from high school. "Our

Sweet Girl Graduate," Grandmama called her, hugging her.

"Good trip?" Grandpapa asked Papa.

"Terrible trip," Mr. Luckie said. "Worst trip ever."

"He says that every year," Mrs. Luckie said. "But it wasn't so bad. The children are bigger and they're a whole lot less trouble. They just take up more room."

"Weather's been good," Grandpapa said. "But the radio says there's a hurricane way down in the Caribbean. . . ."

"We heard it on the car radio," Mrs. Luckie said. "It's early in the season for a hurricane, isn't it?"

"They don't usually amount to much this early," Grandpapa said.

Sam began to head once more toward the water. All the Luckies followed him, and the grandparents, too.

The houses at St. Jerome—all of them old and high-ceilinged and most of them unpainted cypress—were strung out along the top of a grassy bluff overlooking Turtle Harbor. Across the bay was a strip of land, a curving peninsula, Turtle Point, that lay between the bay and the Gulf of Mexico.

The view was familiar to them all—and yet every summer it was new again. St. Jerome was home in a way, and like a new beginning.

You had to admit St. Jerome was nice in its way, Quincy thought, if you weren't forced to come every single summer of your whole entire life. . . .

"It smells good," said Jill.

"It's these wonderful pine trees," Mrs. Luckie said, looking up at them.

"The Motts are here," Grandmama said, "and Molly's been asking for you, Ducky."

9

Quincy shrugged. "Okay," she said.

"Molly's such a nice child," Grandmama said. "And Charlie's boy is here with the Standishes this summer. He's about your age, Sam."

Sam made a face. Any new child sponsored, so to speak, by grandparents, would probably turn out to be a bust and a burden.

"What's that stake down there?" Jill asked, pointing to a stout stick anchored in the sand of the beach. A line went out from it to the water.

"That's my shark line," Grandpapa said. "I put out some bait and throw it out in the channel and sometimes I catch a shark."

"What for?"

"Just to see what I'll catch," Grandpapa said. "A man over at the lagoon by St. Lucy had one and I thought I'd try it over here."

"We've got to get unpacked!" Mr. Luckie said. "Ducky, start opening all the shutters. Sarah, take the sheets upstairs and start making up the beds. Melissa, put the groceries away. Jill, help me get the car unloaded. Sam, borrow Grandmama's lawn mower and start on the grass—if you don't, the Jungle will take over. When we finish, we'll all take the boat down."

Quincy first took her telescope out of the car and placed it carefully in a corner of the screened front porch. Then she started opening the shutters.

When the chores were finished to Mr. Luckie's satisfaction, they all went to the shed behind the house to get the boat and, sweating and panting, they carried it and dragged it down to the water.

It was a wooden sailboat, a catboat, a great tub of a boat,

as Mr. Luckie called it, but the Luckies—all but Quincy, who didn't care—were immensely proud that they'd all progressed past the stage of sailing a Sunfish or a Sailfish and had a real boat that wasn't jut a fiberglass surfboard.

They got the sail down from the living room rafters and brought it down and hoisted it. They were ready for the summer.

Three

The next morning the Luckies' house looked like they'd been there forever. Wet towels hung on the clothesline, and wet bathing suits were draped over the railing on the front porch. Guitars and paint box and camera equipment and needlepoint and typewriters and books were more or less in place.

Mr. Luckie was in the kitchen beaming at some trout Grandpapa had caught and cleaned that very morning.

Mrs. Standish was shelling peas on her front porch, and Quincy waved at her as she walked to Molly Mott's house.

"We're having ice cream tonight, Ducky," Mrs. Standish called out.

"Good," Quincy said. She waved again and hurried on, although she was briefly tempted to stop and maybe get a look at "Charlie's boy." Mr. Charlie Standish was her mother's age, and he had moved to New York and married somebody up there, and there was no telling what his son would be like.

Quincy forgot him by the time she passed the next two

houses, which were empty (the Dukes and the Caldwells were not down yet) and came to Miss Hattie Hawk's house. Miss Hattie Hawk was as old as the Ballews and the Standishes and was an expert birdwatcher. She always wore khaki pants and khaki shirts, and a pair of binoculars was always strung around her neck. She knew where to find edible wild mushrooms and how to clean a live conch, and she knew every bird that flew in the Florida skies.

She had taught Florida history until she retired, and she was an expert on the Spanish expeditions to Florida. Even her dog had an historical name. He was the namesake of LeMoyne, who had accompanied a Spanish expedition to draw pictures of the Indians. This LeMoyne was a Labrador retriever and he loved to swim. Nearly every morning he swam out in the big channel in the middle of Turtle Harbor and played with the porpoises.

Miss Hattie Hawk greeted Quincy from her front porch. "I'm going to make some mayhaw jelly today," she said. "I'll bring you-all some when it's cool."

"Thank you," Quincy said. The Luckies loved mayhaw jelly and couldn't get it in Houston.

She walked on to the Motts' house and collected Molly Mott, who was lying on a cot on the front porch watching her mother and her little brother, Pennington, work on a jigsaw puzzle.

The two girls went down to the dock.

Mrs. Mott and Quincy's mother had been friends when they were children in the nearby town of Azalea, and they took it for granted that Molly and Quincy would be friends, too. Oddly enough, they were.

"We sure are different, though," Molly said that morning as she rubbed suntan lotion on her white skin.

"I know it," Quincy said.

"I would never, never want to take computer programming or astronomy," Molly said, having just heard Quincy's account of what she had really wanted to do that summer.

"What do you want to do?" Quincy asked her with genuine curiosity.

"I like to sit," Molly said. "I like to just sit. I really do. It makes my mother so mad. She yells at me to do something."

"You like to read," Quincy said.

"Not as much as you do," Molly said.

"You can sing," Quincy said.

"Not as good as Jill," Molly said.

"Oh, for heaven's sake, you aren't as old as Jill," Quincy said. "Thank heavens. You know, you do like to sit a lot, don't you? I'm not like that. I don't want to just sit around. What makes me mad is my family doesn't have the faintest interest in anything I'm interested in. They just don't know science exists."

"Nobody's family is interested in what the children want to do," Molly said.

"That's not true," Quincy said. "My parents are all interested in everything Sam and Melissa and Jill like to do. Sam likes photography and music and Melissa is terrific at art and Jill is musical and they all love to act. And my parents are like that, too."

"My mother says you all are very creative," Molly said.

"*They* are all very creative," Quincy said. "Papa teaches English, and his Shakespeare classes are famous—he acts all the parts in the plays in class. And Mama teaches acting."

"You can act," said Molly. "You've always been in the Summer Show."

14

"Well, everybody's always in the Summer Show," Quincy said. "And that's okay if you're little, but now I'm interested in other things besides acting. That's all."

"You were pretty good," Molly said.

"Acting's all right," Quincy said. "I'm not against art and music. I don't want to stamp out everything they're into. It's just that science is so much more interesting than all those things. . . . They just don't understand one teeny bit what I care about. They don't have any idea at all about space or math or physics or anything that's really great at all. They don't even know there's something that they don't know about. They don't care."

They were silent.

"Oh, shoot," Quincy said, "let's go swimming."

"I don't think I want to go yet," Molly said.

Quincy looked around her. It was a perfect June day at St. Jerome. The sun was shining. The water of Turtle Harbor was fairly clear—as clear as it ever got at St. Jerome —and a breeze was blowing so it wasn't too hot. The tide was high so they could dive off the dock. St. Jerome was not such a bad place to be if you couldn't be where there was a library or an observatory or a laboratory. . . .

"Molly, do you know why my mother said she married my father?"

"No, why?" Molly was very interested. This was, in fact, the third summer that Molly and Quincy had pooled all their information on why people got married, what they did before they got married, and what they did after they got married.

"It was because he was going to be a college professor," Quincy said, "and he'd have the summers off so they could come to St. Jerome."

"Hey, that's not so bad," said Molly. "Where's Sam?"

"I don't know," said Quincy. "I guess he took the boat out. And he fools around with those kids up at the end. Come on, let's go swimming."

"I don't think I'll go in," Molly said again.

"Why?"

"I just don't think I will," Molly said.

"Oh, come on," Quincy said.

"I'm not going to go in this summer," Molly said. "On account of the sharks."

"There aren't any sharks in Turtle Harbor," Quincy said.

"There are sharks everywhere," Molly said.

"What's the matter with you, Molly?" Quincy said. "Did you see *Jaws*?"

"I wouldn't see *Jaws* for all the money in the world," said Molly. "I read a book about sharks this winter. It wasn't a story—it was fact. I don't think I'll go in swimming as long as I live. Not even in a pool."

"Molly Mott! Are you going to sit there all summer and not go in swimming?"

"I don't mind sitting. Don't forget that," Molly said.

"Queer," Quincy said.

But she felt a bit uneasy as she dived into the bay and swam toward the channel. Good grief, Molly was dopey. She had those big blue eyes and she stared at you and said the oddest things sometimes.

Quincy climbed out on the dock and saw her mother and Molly's mother walking toward them. St. Jerome was not the kind of resort where people came down and lay on the beach with umbrellas and towels and transistor radios. The beach was too narrow and there was too much sea-

16

weed. And the people who came to St. Jerome just weren't that kind of people anyway—or so they said.

The children all went swimming off the community dock or way out in the bay where the water was deeper. The men usually went fishing. Grandmothers sat on the front porches, and some of the mothers went swimming.

Mrs. Luckie and Mrs. Mott were among those mothers who usually came down to the water, and Mrs. Luckie actually went in. Today she dived off the dock and came to the surface and turned on her back and floated.

"How can you float so long?" Quincy called to her mother.

"It's easy," Mrs. Luckie said, not opening her eyes.

Mrs. Mott sat a while, and then walked back toward her house. Mrs. Luckie finally got out of the water.

"Can Molly come to lunch?" Quincy asked. "Papa's cooking trout."

"Sure," said Mrs. Luckie, starting back toward the house.

"You do remember that my father shouts a lot," Quincy said to Molly. "Don't you?"

"I love it," Molly said. "It's so much more interesting than a quiet father."

Four

At lunch, Mr. Luckie had cooked the trout to perfection and had fried hush puppies to go with it and cooked grits.

"I wish my father could cook," Molly said, as she ate her fourteenth hush puppy.

"Do you know how the hush puppy got its name?" Mr. Luckie asked Molly.

"No, sir," Molly said, looking at him with her blue eyes wide.

Quincy had heard the story a thousand times and she felt sure Molly had, too, but they both listened as Mr. Luckie told it again.

"It started at a big fish fry right around here in North Florida. The men were frying all these fish and everybody was waiting for the fish to get done, and the dogs smelled the fish frying and started howling. One of the men took some cornmeal and made up a little batter and dropped a little in the hot grease where the fish was frying, and then when it was done he threw one of the little fried pieces of corn bread to each of the dogs, and called out, 'Hush, puppy! Hush, puppy!' and that's how the hush puppy got its name."

"They sure are good," Molly said. "No matter how they got their name."

Next to the food, Melissa was the center of attention. She had gone into Elysium, the nearest little town, and gotten herself a job in the Shell Shop, which sold souvenirs and inner tubes as well as shells.

"That's wonderful, Melissa," Quincy said. "That means you won't be here to pick on me."

"That means I'll make a thousand dollars this summer—and I need it to buy some warm clothes before I go off to college. And I can buy new paints. . . ."

"Dammit, it will cost me a thousand dollars to get you to Elysium and back every day," Mr. Luckie said.

"It will all work out," said Mrs. Luckie. "Melissa can drive Grandpapa's car part of the time."

After lunch, Molly and Quincy sat in the big rope hammock on the Luckies' front porch. Mrs. Luckie was working on her needlepoint at the other end of the porch for a while, and then she said, "I give up. I'm going to go take a nap," and left.

"Have you seen Mrs. Standish's grandson?" Molly asked.

"No, I haven't," Quincy said. "I went by there this morning, but I didn't see him. Have you seen him?"

"Yes."

"What's he like?" Quincy asked.

"He's pretty dopey," Molly said. "He's from New York," she added vaguely.

"I never knew anyone actually from New York," Quincy said. "How long is he going to be here?"

"I guess all summer," Molly said.

They swayed back and forth in the hammock for a while. "Do you want to go swimming?" Quincy asked.

"No," said Molly.

"We could go sailing," Quincy said, "but Sam has the boat. Do you want to go fishing?"

"It's awful hot," Molly said. "You know what's fun? Paint-by-number. Do you think somebody would take us into Elysium to get some pictures to paint-by-number?"

"I don't know," Quincy said. "Why don't we just go fishing?"

"Oh, if we go fishing, we have to find the poles and the hooks and the lines and the sinkers and get some bait—and I hate to put bait on the hook." Molly wrinkled her nose in disgust.

"Oh, for heaven's sake, Molly, we have all that stuff. I tell you what. Let's go fishing. You can just sit there on the dock and I'll fish. I might catch me a fish. I'll check the crab traps, too. Sam put them out yesterday evening."

"Okay," said Molly, with something that was close to enthusiasm. "Nobody ever suggested I could just sit before."

"Well, just sit here while I go find the poles. I guess they're all still under the house," Quincy said.

She went out through the kitchen where her father was unloading more groceries. "Oh, Papa, next time you go to town, Molly and I want to go," she said.

"Okay," Mr. Luckie said.

Quincy went out the back door, slamming the screen. She knelt down in the grass by the side of the house and peered underneath. There were the cane poles, stored from last year. She pulled them out and, as usual, several had split during the winter. She picked out the one that looked the sturdiest and found it had a line, a hook, a sinker, and a float, and she started back through the house.

"Did you get any fish bait?" she asked her father.

"In the freezer."

Quincy found a package of frozen bait shrimp in the freezer and went back out to the front porch. "Let's go," she said to Molly, who got up from the hammock and followed her slowly down to the dock.

Molly sat down on the floor of the dock and leaned against a bench. She looked utterly relaxed, utterly happy. Quincy first checked the crab traps, which were big boxes made of wire fencing. Sam had put fish heads in the traps for bait and then lowered the traps into the water at the end of a rope. He had tied the other end of the rope to the dock railing.

There were two crabs in one trap, none in the other.

"I'll put these back down," Quincy said. "Sam can take them out later."

"I hate crab," Molly said.

"I like to eat crab," Quincy said, "but I hate to clean them. This huge old blue crab only has about a teaspoonful of meat, and it's all in his claws. It takes a million crabs to do anything with."

"I just hate the whole idea," Molly said.

Quincy sat down on the edge of the dock with her legs hanging down and waited about two minutes, until the sun thawed a frozen shrimp enough for her to pull it off the ice block and put it on her hook.

She dropped her hook in the water and waited.

She was about to point out to Molly that she might as well sit there with a fishing pole in her hand as well as sit there without one, and then nobody could accuse her of just sitting, but then she remembered that Molly didn't want to bait the hook.

"Here he comes," Molly said.

"Who?" Quincy asked.

"Mrs. Standish's grandson," Molly said.

Quincy turned and looked at the boy who was coming out on the dock. He was, as Grandmama had said, about Sam's age, but he looked not at all like Sam, who was thin and tall and wiry and, Quincy thought, very good-looking.

The Standish grandson was short and pale and had on funny-looking shorts—not cut-off jeans, which was what everybody at St. Jerome always wore—and he wore glasses. He came out on the dock slowly.

"Hello," he said to Molly.

"Hello," she said.

Quincy looked at him, and she suddenly felt sorry for him. He looked miserable, she thought.

"Hi," she said. "My name's Quincy Luckie."

"I'm Mike Standish," he said.

"You're from New York," Quincy said.

"Yes."

"How do you like St. Jerome?"

"The bay is very interesting as a marine nursery," he said.

"What?" Quincy said.

"Turtle Harbor is a remarkable marine nursery," he said. "It's an incubator. All sorts of marine organisms grow here."

"How did you know that?" Quincy said. She was genuinely impressed.

"Observation," Mike said. "You can tell if you look at low tide. You can see the whelks and the cones and the conchs and hermit crabs. You can see the cucumbers in the grass up at Sting Ray Point. You can see the barnacles on the dock pilings. You—"

"What Quincy meant," Molly said, interrupting him,

"was how do you like St. Jerome as a place to stay?"

"That's what I meant," Quincy said, "but go on about the marine nursery. I've seen all those things at low tide, but I never thought about the bay being an incubator."

"It's just that it's protected by land on three sides from surf and wave action," Mike said. "The water temperature is right and there's been no destructive dredging. Optimum conditions have been preserved for marine life."

Molly giggled. "And how do you like it as a place to stay?"

"It's very interesting," Mike said.

"Ow!" said Quincy, pulling up her pole. "Look! I caught an eel!"

"It's not an eel," said Mike. "It's a needlefish. Watch out."

"It's weird-looking," Molly said. She got up off the dock and sat on the bench, her feet tucked under her.

"Oh, for heaven's sake, Molly, it won't hurt you," Quincy said. She began to take the hook out of the needle-fish's mouth. "I'll just throw it back."

"No, give it to me," Mike said. He knelt down and began to pull out the hook. "I want it for my collection."

"Your collection?" Quincy said.

"Yes," Mike said. "I've decided to make a collection of marine specimens this summer. I preserve some in formaldehyde, and I have a saltwater aquarium where I'm trying to keep some alive."

"Ugh," said Molly.

"Did you know much about—er, marine life before this summer?" Quincy asked. "I mean, you haven't been here at St. Jerome before, have you?"

"Not since I was four or five years old," Mike said. "But

my spiritual home in New York is the Museum of Natural History. I intend to be a biologist. Actually, I'm basically more interested in other types of organisms—frogs, lizards, for example—"

Molly said "Ugh!" again, but Mike went right on.

"—but I decided I might as well work with marine life while I'm here."

"How long have you been here?" Quincy asked.

"A couple of weeks. I go to private school, or I did go to private school, and it gets out earlier than public schools. My mother sent me down here right away." He sighed.

He sounded pretty dismal about it, Quincy thought.

"I didn't want to come here either," Quincy said. "I want to be a scientist, too, but I'm interested in astronomy."

"Oh? That takes a great deal of mathematical ability," he said. "I prefer living organisms, myself." He said he'd better be going and he turned and walked away.

Quincy sighed. Was there no one in the world besides herself—and Arthur C. Clarke—who cared about space? Oh, well, she thought. "Hey, Molly," she said, "do you want to come over and look through my telescope tonight?"

"What at?" Molly asked.

"What do you think we'd look at?" Quincy said. "The stars. Or, rather, the planets. The moon. . . ." She stopped. She was reluctant to tell Molly what it was she hoped to see with her telescope—if she put it into words it might sound too crazy even for a friend like Molly. Jupiter and its moons . . . Saturn and its rings . . . better not say it out loud.

"I guess I will," Molly was saying, "since we don't have television."

"I know," Quincy said. "We don't either. And I miss *Star Trek*."

"I miss everything," Molly said. "You ought to hear my mother bragging about St. Jerome. She says, 'And we don't have television. Those people over on Turtle Point have televisions, but then they like motorboats instead of sailboats. . . .'"

"I like motorboats myself," Quincy said.

"I bet they have a lot better time on Turtle Point," Molly said. "I don't think it's all that nice over here. They have surf on the Gulf side, and they have the marina and a store where you can buy ice cream and Cokes. They have television—and some of them have air conditioning."

"Wouldn't you be scared of sharks on Turtle Point, more than you are here?" Quincy asked.

"I couldn't be," Molly said.

They had climbed the steps to the top of the bluff, and Molly turned toward her house.

"Are you coming tonight?" Quincy called.

"Oh, I guess so," Molly said. "What time?"

"When it gets dark," Quincy said.

"Oh," Molly said.

Five

When it began to get dark, Quincy unpacked her telescope and started outside with it.

"Come on, Ducky," Mrs. Luckie said, as Quincy was going out the door. "Are you coming?"

"Where?" Quincy asked.

"Down to the Standishes to eat ice cream," Mrs. Luckie said.

"I forgot," Quincy said. "Can I come later maybe? Molly's coming down here."

"I'm sure the Motts are going over to the Standishes, too," Mrs. Luckie said.

"I want to set up my telescope," Quincy said.

Mrs. Luckie sighed in exasperation. "Oh, all right. But come on down later."

Quincy took the telescope to a cleared space away from the trees and set it up. She began to do all the adjustments outlined in the directions. She consulted her book on stargazing and followed its advice. She adjusted the shortest lens first, then went on to the next.

26

It worked. She was elated—and a little surprised. It worked.

She looked up at the sky without the telescope and spotted Venus, the evening star. Okay. She knelt down and looked through the telescope at the sky. She moved the tube until she found Venus.

When she looked at it through the telescope, its brightness jolted her. It was brilliant, incredibly brilliant, up there in the evening sky.

"Hi."

Quincy jumped. It was Molly.

"Oh, hi, Molly. Come look at Venus."

She showed Molly how to kneel down and where to look.

"I don't see anything," Molly said.

"Wait a minute," Quincy said. "Let me look again." She found Venus again. "Okay, look at it. Quick."

Molly knelt and looked. "It's bright," she said. "Now I've lost it again."

"I'll find it for you," Quincy said.

Molly dutifully looked again. "It is really bright. I've lost it again. Why is that?"

"We're moving," Quincy said. "Don't you know? The earth turns. And Venus is moving, too. We're both hurtling through space."

"You mean we really *are* moving," Molly said. "I never really believed it before."

"Aren't you the one who didn't believe the earth was really round until the astronauts brought back those photographs?" Quincy said.

Molly giggled. "I still think they might have faked those photographs."

"Now let's look at the Big Dipper," Quincy said. "I don't mean the whole thing, but the stars in it. Here, look."

Molly looked. "It looks just like Venus," she said.

"Oh, it does not," Quincy said. "Here, let's look at the moon."

"Let's go get ice cream," Molly said. "I told your mother I'd bring you back."

"Oh, all right. I can come back and look some more," Quincy said.

They were quiet as they walked down toward the Standishes' house. The Standishes, like the Ballews, had always brought their children to St. Jerome for the summers. But now the Standish "children" were all grown and living far away. Charlie Standish, Quincy had learned from Molly, was divorcing his wife, and so Mike had been "sent" to St. Jerome for the summer.

Quincy thought about this as she walked down the little cement walk. Would it be worse to be "sent" off to your grandparents at St. Jerome for the summer, or was it worse to have to come with your whole family?

It might be fun to come and stay with Grandmama and Grandpapa, Quincy thought. You'd at least have peace and quiet.

Everybody was sitting on the Standishes' front porch and front steps, eating ice cream.

"Come in, come in, Ducky Luckie," Mr. Standish said. "Have you met Mike?"

"Yes, sir," Quincy said. "I met him on the dock this afternoon."

"Have some vanilla ice cream, Ducky. And Molly, you have some, too. Notice I didn't say have some *more* ice cream. I said, have *some* ice cream. We never count seconds on ice cream. If we did, my wife would split my head open."

Molly and Quincy got bowls of ice cream and sat down on the steps with the other young people and children. The grown-ups sat in the rocking chairs on the porch, and the children were quiet while the grown-ups talked—and talked pointlessly, it seemed to Quincy.

"Mmmmm . . . this is good ice cream. . . ."

". . . but you know, I don't believe it's as good when you make it in an electric ice cream freezer as it was when we used the old hand-turned churn. . . ."

"It can't be any different just because electricity turns the handle instead of elbow grease. . . ."

"But it is different! And I used the same recipe. . . ."

"It's delicious, Mrs. Standish. It couldn't be better."

"Remember how hard it used to be to get ice down here?"

"The ice man used to drive down from Elysium once a week, or maybe once every two weeks. The kids would see him and start to holler, 'The ice man's coming. . . .' "

"And we'd have an ice cream social that night for sure!"

"Everybody would come and sit on somebody's front steps and we'd sing."

"We don't sing like we used to do, do we?"

"The prettiest thing to me was when we used to go sailing at night . . . maybe two boats out in the bay . . . all full of us young people"—Quincy noted that this was her grandfather, her *grandfather*, who was seventy-five, talking—"and the people in each boat would be singing and you could see the phosphorescence in the water and one boat would sail near the other and you'd hear the people in the other boat singing, and it was the prettiest thing I ever heard. . . ."

"It certainly is nice to sit here, isn't it, and look out over the water at the lights on Turtle Point?"

29

"I feel so safe here. You know, one good hurricane would blow them away over there on Turtle Point."

"What happened to that little hurricane . . . Alberta . . . that was down in the Caribbean?"

"Still there. Moving mighty slow. Won't amount to much, I expect," said Quincy's grandfather.

Quincy got up.

"Where are you going, Ducky?" asked her mother.

"I'm going back down to my telescope," Quincy said.

"Oh, don't run off," Mrs. Luckie said. "We're about to talk about the Summer Show."

"You don't need me," Quincy said.

"We need everybody," Mrs. Luckie said.

"Even you, Duck-brain," Sam said.

"What are you going to look at with your telescope?" Grandmama asked.

What does she think I'm going to look at? Quincy wondered. Honestly! "You know," she said vaguely, "Venus. And I want to find Jupiter and Saturn. . . ." Why did they make her feel guilty? "I'm just *learning* about it," she said. "I just started. Give me a break."

"All you Luckie people are so *creative*," said Molly's mother.

Molly punched Quincy, and Quincy punched her back. Quincy started to leave again.

"Don't go," said Mrs. Luckie.

"What are you going to do for the Summer Show this year?" Mrs. Mott asked.

"I don't know yet," Mrs. Luckie said.

"I liked it the year we did the dream sequence from Shakespeare," said Jill. "You know, *Midsummer Night's Dream* and *Macbeth*."

30

"That was pretty, all right," Mrs. Luckie said, "but somehow I don't think it was the most popular thing we ever did."

"I kind of liked the time you did that short version of *Sound of Music*," said Grandmama.

"That turned out better than I thought it would," Mrs. Luckie said. "Jill was Maria, and she was good, and everybody helped. Molly and Quincy were good."

"*Charlie Brown* was good," said Mrs. Mott.

"Yeah, Melissa was typecast," said Quincy. "She was Lucy."

"Why don't we write our own script this time?" Melissa said.

"And do our own songs!" Jill said.

"Oh, that would be marvelous," Mrs. Luckie said. "Do you think we could?"

Quincy's heart sank. What a lot of bother that would be, she thought. Oh, good grief, they'd never stop talking about that. But Jill and Melissa were rattling on now about how "relevant" it would be.

"You all are so *creative*!" said Mrs. Mott again. Quincy poked Molly again.

"We need a story line," Melissa said authoritatively.

"We could do Turtle Harbor itself," said Mike Standish eagerly. "We could make it an ecological drama, and the characters could be the porpoises and the stingrays and the mullet and the hermit crabs."

Dead silence met this suggestion, until Melissa said sharply, "That sounds terrible."

"It's something to think about," Mrs. Luckie said tactfully. "Don't discourage *any* ideas at this stage of the game."

Quincy felt horribly sorry for Mike. He had tried to

31

enter into the spirit of the thing—and look what had happened. Melissa had squelched him, and her mother hadn't been much better.

"Come on, Mike," she said, "let's go look at stars. Come on, Molly."

"I think I'll just sit here," Molly said.

"*Come on*," Quincy said between clenched teeth. "Come on."

Cowed, Molly got up and followed Mike and Quincy down the path.

"Gosh, they make me sick," Quincy said. "Them and their old Summer Show."

"I think it's kind of an interesting project," Mike said. "Myself, I'm not gifted verbally, not as gifted as I am cognitively, so I'm afraid I won't be much help. But it's rather interesting that your family takes on this project summer after summer."

Quincy was surprised. Mike didn't seem to be at all upset that his crummy idea had been rejected. Instead, he seemed able to look about him, observing the people and their activities as he might observe a fish in an aquarium.

A phrase leaped to her mind: scientific detachment. Did Mike have scientific detachment?

"I guess it is impressive," she said, "but it gets kind of boring, summer after summer, the way they get so excited about the Show, I mean."

They were now at the telescope. Venus was gone. Quincy focused on the moon and let Mike look.

"It is bright, isn't it?" he said, getting up.

Quincy was disappointed. Was that all he was going to say about the *moon*, and the way it looked through the telescope?

"I'd rather look at creatures through a microscope," Mike said, as if he could read her thoughts.

Quincy knelt down to look at the moon again. She should run get the book and try to find Jupiter . . . but Mike and Molly were distracting her.

"I can't get all your family straight," Mike was saying. "You have two sisters?"

"Two sisters and a brother," Quincy said. "Melissa is the oldest. She just graduated from high school. Jill is sixteen."

"Jill is nicer than Melissa," Molly said.

"Well, she's not as bad as Melissa—put it like that," Quincy said. "Melissa is the one that jumped on you about the Show. She has long black hair. Jill has curly hair."

"And your brother's name is Sam?" Mike asked.

"That's right," Quincy said.

"How old is he?" Mike asked.

"He's fourteen," Quincy said.

"That's how old I am," Mike said, "but he seems younger."

"That's because he plays around. He likes to sail and swim. He's a good photographer, and he and both my sisters play the guitar."

"You have a very unusual family," Mike said.

"You said it," Quincy said, ignoring the note of envy she heard in Mike's voice.

Six

When Quincy got up the next morning, her father offered to fix her some breakfast. This was unusual. At St. Jerome, everybody just ate breakfast any old time.

"How about some sausage and eggs?" Mr. Luckie said. "Or some pancakes?"

"Oh, all right, pancakes," Quincy said without enthusiasm. She went out on the front porch and looked to see if LeMoyne was out in the bay playing with the porpoises. She could see neither dog nor porpoises.

"What's the matter with you, Ducky?" her father asked when she came back in the kitchen.

"Nothing. Why?"

"Now, look here, Ducky, I don't want you to spoil everybody's summer. You'll break your mother's heart if you don't help with the Summer Show. You know how crazy she is about it."

"Oh, Papa, do I have to help with the Summer Show every summer? It seems—I don't know . . . I just get tired of talking about it all the time."

Her father was watching the pancakes on the griddle carefully. But he kept on talking to her. "You know how much the Show means to your mother, Ducky," he said.

"I know," Quincy said. "I guess I know. But I'm interested in other things now."

Her father, waiting to turn the pancakes, glanced out the window. "Hmmm. A few clouds today," he said.

Quincy got up from the table and looked out at the sky. "You know," she said, glad to change the subject, "you think of clouds as being very ordinary things. But actually they're like something out of science fiction—dust and vapor and huge."

"Listen, Ducky," Mr. Luckie said. He flipped her pancakes onto a plate and handed her the plate with a flourish. He pushed the butter and syrup toward her and sat down across the table from her and leaned forward intently. "Listen, that science stuff. You know, I used to think I was interested in mathematics and science when I was your age. I wanted to go to Georgia Tech and study architectural engineering."

Quincy looked at him.

"But I outgrew it," he said triumphantly. "And you'll outgrow it, too."

I will *not* outgrow it, Quincy thought grimly, chewing her pancakes.

"There, that's settled," her father said. "More pancakes?"

She was tempted briefly to tell her father she didn't want pancakes cooked by such an un-understanding father—but she thought better of it. "Sure," she said.

When Melissa was about to leave for her job in Elysium, Quincy asked her if she'd get two paint-by-number pictures for her and Molly.

"No! That's the worst thing I ever heard of," Melissa said. "Never in a million years would I get anybody any paint-by-number pictures. They're a disgrace to Art."

"Oh, for heaven's sake, don't be so high and mighty!" said Quincy. "We like paint-by-number." Quincy really didn't care whether she had any paint-by-number pictures or not, but Molly wanted them, and, loyally, Quincy decided to put up a fight for them.

"You two should learn to express yourselves and create your own images and impressions," Melissa said.

"But we don't want to do that," Quincy said. "We just want to fool around with paint-by-number."

"You are such a baby!" Melissa said.

Quincy tried to decide whether to appeal the matter to her parents. She hated to use phrases like "Mama, make her do so and so," or "Papa, tell her to do such and such," and she considered them beneath her.

As if she could read Quincy's mind, Mrs. Luckie intervened. "Melissa, get them each one paint-by-number," she said. "It won't stunt their artistic development." Mrs. Luckie turned to Quincy. "Right now, Ducky, come walk on the beach with me, will you? I haven't been down to Sting Ray Point yet, have you? Come on, let's go."

Quincy said all right and the two of them set out. After they'd left the St. Jerome houses behind and were alone on the empty beach, Mrs. Luckie took Quincy's hand.

"Ducky, is something the matter?" she asked.

"What do you mean—is something the matter?" Quincy said. She took her hand away.

"Well, you seem sort of cranky and I thought maybe something was troubling you," Mrs. Luckie said.

"Nothing's troubling me except that I didn't want to

36

come to the beach. I wanted to go to summer school at Rice and I want to learn about astronomy and computer science. Nobody in this family cares one bit about me. Everybody just wants me to be like everybody else and be a great dramatic machine or something and just do what everybody else wants to do."

Quincy was surprised at her own anger, but she couldn't stop. "The rest of you are all alike. And I don't try to stop anybody from anything they want to do. But once in a while I'd like to do what I want to do," Quincy finished.

"Ducky-baby, I can't stand it!" Mrs. Luckie was genuinely upset, Quincy could see. "Are we really so cruel? I didn't know you didn't want to come to the beach—I didn't know you wanted to go to Rice so bad until just a day before we left home. You know I don't want you to be just like everybody else. You know your father and I want each of you children to be free, to be an individual. But you'll have to tell me ahead of time about things you want to do."

"It wouldn't make any difference. Nobody ever listens."

"Ducky!"

"Nobody listens," Quincy said. "You never listen. I tell you about things and you just tune me out. I tell you about Arthur C. Clarke and you don't hear me. Sometimes I tell you something wild, like 'I just drowned Sam in the bathtub,' and you just smile and nod and say, 'Good.' "

"Oh, Ducky, I don't!"

"You do."

"Ducky, I promise you we'll try to do better. But you must help, too. Try to cooperate and be one of the family. Take part in things. And help with the Show. You know how much your father enjoys the Summer Show. Your

37

father enjoys it more than anything else at the beach, so we must all work together to make it top-notch. You know how angry and hurt he'd be if you didn't help with it."

"Why? Mama, why should anybody be upset if I didn't help with the Show? Why?"

They had stopped walking and they were standing on the beach facing one another. Mrs. Luckie reached for Quincy's hand again. This time Quincy let her hold it, and they began to walk again.

"I don't know why it would upset him so if you didn't help," Mrs. Luckie said. "I honestly don't know. But it would. Maybe because it would mean the end of the family, or something. Even the older kids keep on helping with it, and if you—the baby—quit, I guess it would mean the family was breaking up. It would mean old age and the end of life—"

"Good grief!" Quincy said.

"I guess it is silly," Mrs. Luckie said. "But come on and help us, won't you?"

"Can't you just forget about me for a while? Can't I just look in my telescope without going to a meeting about the Show? Can't I read Arthur C. Clarke if I want to? Can't I go to the library if I want to?"

"We'll try," Mrs. Luckie said. "And you try, too. Fair enough?"

They were at Sting Ray Point and they began to slide their feet through the shallow water, being very careful, but looking for rays. Quincy realized nobody had really promised anything to anybody.

At lunch, Quincy caused another small uproar.

Somebody asked her what she wanted for her birthday, which wasn't until August, anyway.

"I want a motorboat," she said quickly.

A storm of disbelief broke.

"Ducky, you are an anomaly in this family," Jill said. She sounded rather admiring.

"What does anomaly mean?" Quincy said.

"Go look it up," Mrs. Luckie said. It was a rule in the Luckie family that if you didn't know the meaning of a word, you went straight to the dictionary to look it up. "That way you'll always remember what it means," Mrs. Luckie had explained over and over.

It always amazed the Luckies' friends that they had so many dictionaries. There were even three at the beach. Quincy looked in the one in the living room.

"Anomaly: Deviation from the common rule, type, or form."

Quincy felt rather proud. She didn't mind being an anomaly in this family, she decided.

"Imagine wanting a motorboat—we're a sailing family," Jill said.

"Grandpapa has a motorboat," Quincy said. "A big one."

"That's different," Jill said. "He's old."

"Why do you want a motorboat?" Mr. Luckie asked her.

"I like motors," Quincy said. "I really do. And you don't have to fool around with tacking, and they don't capsize. I really would like to have a little boat this summer, with just a tiny little motor. It doesn't have to be big enough to ski behind."

Seven

The next day they had to evacuate St. Jerome.

The weather was still sunny when Quincy got up, but after breakfast two men from the Florida Department of Public Safety came to the back door and told Mr. and Mrs. Luckie that everybody would have to leave St. Jerome.

"Alberta's gotten bigger, and she's moving faster," one of the officers said. "We're evacuating the whole coast."

"But, Officer, we've never left St. Jerome because of a hurricane before. The bluff protects these houses. Now, over there on Turtle Point—that's another story. They're right at sea level, and they're vulnerable," Mrs. Luckie said.

"I'm sorry, ma'am," said the officer, "but we're asking everybody to leave."

"We never left when I was a little girl," Mrs. Luckie said. "We'd stay right here. Of course, we didn't know when a hurricane was coming in those days. But we never got hurt. I remember my mother and Aunt Gussie were down here with just us children, and there was a bad storm—

40

I guess we'd call it a hurricane now. The next morning Papa and Uncle George came down from Azalea to see about us. They said they had to stop and saw up five trees that had blown down across the road. We were all so excited, we put salt in the coffee."

The officers smiled at Mrs. Luckie's reminiscence, but they were firm. Everybody had to leave St. Jerome.

Grandmama and Grandpapa came over and said for the Luckies to come on up to Azalea and stay with them. "It's a good thing we didn't sell that old barn of a house like you wanted to," Grandmama said to Grandpapa. "Where would we put everybody now?"

"I hate to leave," said Mrs. Luckie, "but I guess we have to."

"These houses have been here a long time," said Grandpapa. "I think we'd be all right, but I guess it's best not to take any chances."

Quincy was rather excited. "It's like *Rendezvous with Rama*," she said to Jill.

"What's that?" Jill asked.

"It's a book by Arthur C. Clarke," Quincy said.

"Oh."

Everybody began to pack up. The question was, what should they take? Quincy wanted, of course, to take her telescope, and everybody else wanted to take everything they owned, too. Finally, Mr. Luckie issued an edict: nothing but clothes for one night, or, at the most, two nights. "That's all," he said.

"If the storm washes the houses away," he said, "we're just wiped out. That's all."

Quincy went down to the dock and was surprised at how rough the water was. The waves were high indeed for

Turtle Harbor, tossing madly, with white foam on the top of each wave. It looked almost like surf rolling in to the beach.

Mike Standish was on the beach. "I wonder what the storm will do to marine life," he said. "I would certainly like to stay and watch it." He sighed heavily.

"Do you really think the hurricane will hit here?" Quincy asked him.

"It is impossible to determine the course of a hurricane," he said.

"I know *that*," Quincy said. "But what do you *think*?"

"I don't know," he said. "If it comes in anywhere near here, Turtle Point is in trouble."

"It *would* be fun to see a hurricane," Quincy said. "But then it might be dangerous."

She went by the Motts' house to see Molly and found Molly sitting in her mother's car.

"What are you doing, Molly?" Quincy asked, peering through the window.

"I'm ready to go," Molly said. "I hate storms."

"There's no need to be scared yet," Quincy said.

"I don't care," Molly said. "I just want to get away from here."

Molly's mother came out of the house carrying a suitcase. "Just let me find your brother, Molly," she said, "and we'll be on our way."

"Keep a stiff upper lip, Molly," Quincy said. She walked away wondering what that phrase meant. It seemed to her that it was more important to keep a stiff lower lip—it was your lower lip that always quivered in giveaway fashion when you were frightened or about to cry under disgraceful circumstances.

By the time the Luckies got packed and ready to leave, the sky was cloudy, and it was beginning to rain a little.

Waiting out the hurricane in Azalea wasn't so bad. The day was hot and humid, and the air was quite still. It began to pour down rain in town soon after they got there, and the wind began to blow a little later.

Quincy borrowed her grandmother's transparent plastic raincoat, her plastic scarf, and her plastic rain boots—and then her library card—and went to the library. She checked out two books by Arthur C. Clarke and a book about quasars. It looked fascinating, and she was quite pleased as she trudged back to her grandmother's house in the rain. If they had to stay two days in Azalea, it wouldn't be so bad.

Her father and mother went around buying up supplies in case the town was hit by the hurricane . . . lots of bread and canned foods. Her grandfather put adhesive tape on all the windows. Her grandmother drew a tubful of water, in case the water supply was cut off.

They all had a good hot supper that her grandmother and her father cooked together, chatting amiably in the kitchen as they worked. Then they moved into the sitting room to watch the television and follow the storm's progress.

The hurricane moved faster for a while, then it slowed down, then it veered off to the west. At this point, the Luckies began to peel off one by one and go to bed.

Quincy and her grandfather stayed up, however, and toward morning they learned Alberta had turned back toward the panhandle of North Florida and had picked up speed as well.

The Azalea television station announced its crews were

leaving the coastal areas for safety as the hurricane drew nearer. Elysium, they said, was shut up tighter than a tick.

The rain outside was hard.

There was no authoritative, on-the-spot news for some time just before daylight. Quincy and Mr. Ballew hung on, though, listening to both the radio and the television. One by one, the other members of the family got up to rejoin them.

Then the report came that Alberta had indeed struck with full force at Turtle Point and had then skipped back out to sea. Azalea was not going to be hit—except by torrential rains. But what about St. Jerome? No news from St. Jerome.

Quincy went to bed and slept.

Eight

The rains began to slow down about lunch time, and the Luckies and the Ballews decided to go back down to the coast.

The radio and television reports still hadn't mentioned St. Jerome.

"It's too small for them to notice," said Mrs. Luckie.

Damage to property on Turtle Point was heavy—at least twenty houses wiped out by the high tide, others damaged by wind, boats smashed, docks destroyed, trees down.

In the car on the way down, the Luckies listened to the radio and heard repeated accounts of the damage on Turtle Point. Nobody had been injured, though.

"I do wish they'd say something about St. Jerome," Mrs. Luckie said.

"I expect the bluff's all right," Mr. Luckie said. "Those houses have been there a long time."

As they got closer to the coast, they began to see more signs of the storm—trees down . . . a barn with its roof gone . . . an unsettled, unswept look to the world.

45

Storekeepers in Elysium were taking the adhesive tape off their store windows.

When they turned off the paved road into the Jungle, a fallen tree blocked the road.

"Everybody out," said Mr. Luckie. "Let's see if we can move it."

"It's just like the time my father and Uncle George came down to see about us after the storm when I was a little girl," Mrs. Luckie said with satisfaction.

"I hope St. Jerome's all right," Jill said.

Two more trees on the Jungle road had to be moved. All in all, the Luckies felt they were hacking their way back to St. Jerome under great odds.

When they got to St. Jerome, there was an awful lot of debris lying around. The lawns in front of the houses were covered with a conglomeration of seaweed, tree limbs, boards from docks and boats, and there was an odd hat, a plastic cooler chest, and a few objects that were unrecognizable.

The beach below the bluff was like a garbage dump, with tons of seaweed and driftwood and jetsam of all kinds.

"Millions of seashells," Quincy said.

And the dock was gone.

"Oh, my God!" It wasn't just the loss of the dock, Mr. Luckie explained, but the prospect of getting it rebuilt that disturbed him. "The dock committee will take forever and have a thousand meetings before they get it rebuilt," he said.

The air was sparkling clean, and the sun was shining. The bright, clean air made the mess on the beach and on the bluff look all the more shocking.

Mike Standish was down on the beach with two buckets, picking up something.

"Beachcombing?" asked Quincy.

"I'm gathering specimens," he said haughtily.

"What washed up?" Quincy asked him.

"A great many things," he said, picking up an odd-looking creature, putting it in his bucket, and moving on.

"What's that?" Quincy asked him.

"Sea squirt," he said.

"What's this?"

"Worm tube," he said.

"This?"

"Clam. Don't you know anything?"

"I thought I did," Quincy said. "I've seen pieces of these tubes before and I didn't know what they were." The worm tubes looked like big, curved spaghetti twisted in odd shapes.

"This is a sea cucumber," Mike said. And he added, almost reluctantly, as though he hated to tell her, "I can sell these."

"Sell them? Where?"

"I called this laboratory supply house I know in New York. And they said they could use all I could send. I'll ship them in plastic bags full of seawater, and I'll get two cents apiece for them."

"Gosh," was all Quincy could say. She was awestruck. Mike was really smart, smarter than anybody else around.

"Look at all the cockles," Mike said. He pointed at the double shells speckled in brown and white that lay on the beach. Lots of them were still alive, and the creature that lived inside would stick out a muscular, tough-looking "foot" and propel itself back toward the water of the bay.

"You mean these are real cockleshells?" Quincy asked. "Like Mistress Mary Quite Contrary had?"

"I don't know about Mistress Mary," Mike said. "But a

cockle is any bivalve mollusk of the genus Cardium—or related genera. A cockle has convex radially ribbed valves. This is what is known as the common cockle. As a matter of fact, 'cockle' comes from the word 'coquille'—the French for 'scallop.' "

The trouble with people who knew anything, Quincy thought, is that they always tell you more than you want to know.

Mike was looking at her. "It's hard to see how you could have spent every summer here and not know more about the creatures that live here," he said.

"I thought I knew a lot," said Quincy humbly. "I know sand dollars and I know the difference between a whelk and a conch, and most people don't know that. I know moon shells and angel ray clams and angel wings and augers and things like that. I just never saw this many cockleshells before—well, actually, I didn't know they were cockles."

"The storm washed them up," Mike said.

"We use cockleshells for ash trays," Quincy said.

"And you want to be a scientist," Mike said. He was walking on down the beach now.

"Some scientists are interested in something besides sea creatures," Quincy said. "And I don't see anything so bad about using a cockleshell for an ash tray. We pick the shells up empty, after the creature has died, not when they're alive like these."

"I guess there's nothing wrong with using a shell for an ash tray," Mike said, as they walked down the beach, heads down, looking. "But you should know about the life that's all around you."

"I guess you're right," Quincy said. "But I think you should be more interested in the planets and the stars."

"Everybody can't be an authority on everything," Mike said.

"Exactly," Quincy said.

"Touché," Mike said, stopping to look at her solemnly. "Where are your sisters and brother?" he asked.

"Sam is taking pictures of the storm damage, and Jill is making notes for him of what he takes and where," Quincy said.

"That's a valid contribution to local history," Mike said.

"I guess so," Quincy said. Mike was certainly always interested in what the Luckie children were doing.

He had started back down the beach, picking up sea cucumbers. Quincy followed, occasionally stopping to pick up an unusual shell or piece of coral. She didn't keep much, but she couldn't help looking.

She saw something that glinted gold and stooped down to pick it up. It was flat, with a molded design on it, about the size of a quarter but not round. It was irregular around the edges. What was it?

She rubbed it on her shorts, looked at it again, rubbed it some more. The gold was shining.

"Mike!" she called. "Mike!"

Mike turned around. "What is it?"

"I don't know. Come here." She looked up at him. "I think," she said, "it's an old Spanish coin."

Mike looked at her and then took the gold object and looked at it and then back at her. "What do you mean, an old Spanish coin?"

"Pieces of eight," she said.

The words sounded like magic as she spoke them.

"You know," she said, "maybe it's pirate gold."

He looked at her in disbelief.

"Really?" he said. "What makes you think that?"

"It's gold, isn't it?" she said. "What else could it be?"

"I don't know," Mike said. "Has anybody found one before?"

"I never heard of it if they did," Quincy said.

"Maybe it is," Mike said slowly.

"Let's look for more," Quincy said.

They walked along the beach slowly, heads down, watching carefully. Mike picked up sea cucumbers as they went. They found two more coins—if they were indeed coins—stamped with the same design but still irregularly shaped.

Once Quincy picked up a broken piece of blue-and-white china and looked at it. Something teased her memory as she stared at it. What was it? Something about china. . . . She couldn't remember, and she dropped the fragment on the sand and went on looking for coins.

Sam came to call Quincy. "Papa wants you," he said.

She left reluctantly. Mike's buckets were full, and he decided to go back to the house, too. "See you later," he said. "We'll look some more."

"Okay," Quincy said.

"Got a boyfriend?" Sam asked her.

"No," said Quincy. "Look what I found." She showed him the three pieces of gold.

"What are they?" Sam asked.

"I think they're Spanish coins," Quincy said.

"Really?" Sam handed them back to her.

Quincy showed them to her father, but he was in a hurry and scarcely noticed them.

"We have to get to work," he said. "Everybody's got to help clean up the yard and get rid of this junk. We can haul most of it off to the dump. Save the driftwood for firewood.

Anything that looks like somebody might want it back—a paddle or anything—keep it here by the house. We'll put a notice on the bulletin board in the post office in Elysium about it. Come on, Ducky, we all have to help."

Mr. Luckie wandered about shouting orders, encouragement, and reprimands at everyone as they set to work on the yard. ("No, Sam, don't put that stuff in that pile. . . .")

As they were about to finish, Mr. Luckie made them all groan when he said, "When we finish this yard and our part of the beach, then we'll help your grandmother and grandfather."

Grandpapa appeared and said that certainly would be nice, as he was getting too old to lift and carry. Besides, he had to go to a meeting of the dock committee, and so did Mr. Luckie.

"The dock committee! Oh, good God!" said Mr. Luckie. "There goes forty hours of discussion and argument! I want off the dock committee!"

"Oh, it won't take so long," Grandpapa said. "And we need some young blood on that committee. We old geezers don't know what to do." He looked up at Mr. Luckie from under his hat brim as he lit his pipe.

Quincy, who was dragging a tree branch toward the back yard, looked at her grandfather and wondered if he liked to tease her father to make him lose his temper.

"Oh, you enjoy that fool dock committee!" Mr. Luckie said. "I have better things to do with my time."

"Why don't you put women on the dock committee?" Mrs. Luckie asked.

"Oh, then we never would stop talking," Mr. Luckie said. "Okay, I'll be there. What time is the meeting?"

"About four, I think," Grandpapa said. "I guess we'll

51

have to decide what we want to do and then go talk to Mr. Bite and find how much he'll charge to build it back."

"And then we'll have to come back and talk some more and decide what we can do and can't do," Mr. Luckie said. "I'd rather go to the penitentiary than go to those meetings."

After they'd finished cleaning up the yard, Mrs. Luckie said she'd drive them over to Turtle Point to look at the storm damage.

The damage was, quite simply, horrifying. "It's awful just to see blank places where houses used to be," Jill said. "Look, that's where the Searcy house was. Right there. And it's gone."

The marina appeared to be all right. "That's a miracle," said Mrs. Luckie.

But in most places the destruction and the piles of rubbish were so dismaying that they agreed they shouldn't complain about just having to clean up their yard.

They turned around and went home.

Nine

Quincy woke up early and lay in bed on the upstairs sleeping porch, watching the reflection of the water on the ceiling. The dapples of sunlight and shadow always fascinated her.

And while she lay there, she thought about the coins, for she was sure they were coins. Were they pirate gold?

The person who might know was Miss Hattie Hawk. Why hadn't she thought of Miss Hattie Hawk before?

She got up and got dressed—a simple matter at St. Jerome, since all she did was put on her bathing suit with a shirt over it. She put the coins in her shirt pocket and went downstairs.

She sat on the front porch and watched LeMoyne and the porpoises and ate her cereal, and then she set out.

She stopped off first next door at her grandmother's. Mrs. Ballew was knitting.

"Has Grandpapa checked the shark line yet?" Quincy asked.

"I think he's fixing to go down there now," Mrs. Ballew

said. So Quincy went inside and sat down beside her, and they rocked companionably.

"Whose afghan is that?" Quincy asked.

Mrs. Ballew was knitting an afghan for each of her grandchildren, starting with the oldest, Melissa, and working downward. Since she had ten grandchildren and Quincy was one of the youngest, it would be a long time before she got to her. But Quincy checked every now and then to see how far down the chain Mrs. Ballew had gotten.

"This is Sam's," Mrs. Ballew said. "I'm going to put a tripod on it. Then I have to make one for your Cousin Lucy and one for Butch, and then I'll start on yours."

"What are you going to put on mine?" Quincy asked.

"A duck?" said Mrs. Ballew.

"Oh, Grandmama!" Quincy was horrified.

"What's the matter?"

"I hate that nickname, Ducky," said Quincy.

"You do? I think it's cute. I didn't know you hated it. But what do you want me to embroider on your afghan?"

"A telescope—with Galileo looking through it," Quincy said.

"I could do the telescope, I guess," said Mrs. Ballew. "But I might have a little trouble with Galileo. How about some stars?"

"That would be super," said Quincy. "In blue and gold?"

Mr. Ballew came out on the porch, and he and Quincy set out for the beach. Grandpapa pulled in the shark line— it took a while to haul it in—and there was a large fish on the end. A very large, ugly fish.

"What is it?" she asked.

"It's a sand shark," Grandpapa said. They stood looking down at the shark.

"Is it a killer?" Quincy asked.

"No. Least I never heard of one attacking anybody. They stay down on the bottom of the channel—out in deep water." He kept on staring down at the fish.

"What are you going to do with it?" Quincy asked.

"I guess I'll have to kill it," he said. "Then I'll tie a hitch around its tail and tow it out with the boat and dump it in deep water."

Mr. Ballew took out his knife and cut the shark's throat. It was all Quincy could do to keep from acting like Molly and saying "Ugh." It wouldn't be scientific to say "Ugh." But why did her grandfather bother with the old shark line? she wondered. If he caught a shark every day, it still wouldn't clean out the bay. So why worry about it? But then, why not? It was kind of interesting to see what would turn up every day.

" 'Bye, Grandpapa," she said, and set out for Miss Hattie Hawk's house.

Miss Hattie Hawk was sitting on her front porch, drinking coffee and eating biscuits and mayhaw jelly. Her binoculars were at her elbow.

"Good morning, Quincy," Miss Hattie Hawk said. "Come in. Have some biscuits. Would you like a glass of milk?"

"No, thank you. I mean, no milk. I'd love a biscuit," Quincy said.

"What are you up to this summer?" Miss Hattie Hawk asked.

"Oh, this and that," Quincy said. She didn't know how to get started. But why not just bust out with it? "Were there any pirates around here, ever?"

"No," said Miss Hattie Hawk. She drank some coffee.

"Not at all?" Quincy asked.

"Not at all," Miss Hattie Hawk said. "In fact, there is not a single documented case of piracy in Florida."

"Not at all?" Quincy said again.

"Not at all," Miss Hattie Hawk said again.

"But what about José Gaspar and Gasparilla?" Quincy asked. "And all those tales of buried treasure?"

"Pure fiction," Miss Hattie Hawk said. "The people in Tampa had to make up José Gaspar in order to have a Gasparilla festival. Several competent historians have researched the matter thoroughly, and there is not one single bit of evidence that a pirate ever operated out of any place in Florida."

"But—but . . ." Quincy was at a total loss. All her life she'd heard tales of pirates in Florida. "But what about all those little booklets they sell at places like the Shell Shop?" she asked. "All about pirates in Florida?"

"Pure fiction, I tell you," Miss Hattie Hawk said. "There's not a word of truth in them. They're written by opportunists to make a fast buck."

Quincy was sitting in one of Miss Hattie Hawk's high-backed rocking chairs. They sat side by side facing the bay, watching the gulls. Only they weren't gulls, Quincy had to remind herself. It was Miss Hattie Hawk who had shattered that myth, too, several years ago when she had informed the Luckies that those white seabirds they called gulls were really terns. The jaw of every Luckie had dropped.

"I never knew that," Mrs. Luckie had said, "and I've been coming here all my life."

"I don't care how long you've been coming here, Sarah," Miss Hattie Hawk had said, without rancor, "they're terns, not gulls."

"How did you learn so much about birds?" Quincy had asked Miss Hattie Hawk that day.

"I got a book and studied it," Miss Hawk had said. "Best way in the world to learn anything."

So there were no pirates in Florida, Quincy thought, and there never had been.

She did not doubt for one minute that Miss Hattie Hawk was absolutely right. She always was. But she had to think about this for a minute or two.

Miss Hattie Hawk spread butter and mayhaw jelly on another biscuit and began to eat it. She passed the plate to Quincy, who shook her head. She felt too depressed to eat.

"Then there's no buried treasure—there couldn't be any buried treasure around here, could there?" Quincy asked.

"Not likely," Miss Hattie Hawk said. "Now, the Spaniards were all around here, you know. They named St. Jerome and St. Lucy and St. Marks and St. James and all the places around here. The Narváez expedition marched up from Tampa to right over here by St. Marks. They camped there and built boats to try to get back to Spain. But they certainly didn't bury any treasure. They were almost wiped out. They had to use their shirts to make sails and they had to beat up their stirrups and spurs to make nails to build the boats. De Soto came and found the forge where Narváez and his men had worked. . . ."

Once Miss Hattie Hawk got started on Florida history, it was hard to stop her.

Quincy was profoundly disappointed. She had always had a secret conviction that there was buried treasure at St. Jerome. She knew the Spanish had been all over the place, and she had even daydreamed that she would find the treasure, and that her discovery would be based on scientific knowledge and rational thought. The stumps that

57

marred the beach on the way down to Sting Ray Point were evidence, she knew, that the coast had eroded there, that dry land had once extended much farther out into the bay. Therefore, she had made a mental note that if she ever came upon a map or directions for finding buried treasure, she would remember to interpret the directions in light of the great chunk of coastline that must have washed away in the past four hundred years. A cache that was two hundred furlongs from the water in 1550 would be much nearer the water today, for instance.

It was very depressing to realize that her secret piece of logical reasoning was not going to be useful to her now. Not in the immediate future, anyway.

"Why did you ask about pirates?" Miss Hattie Hawk asked.

Quincy silently fished the gold pieces out of her pocket and handed them to Miss Hattie Hawk. Miss Hattie Hawk looked at them carefully and then looked up at Quincy.

"These are Spanish coins," she said. "See the cross on one side and the head of King Philip on the other? They are doubloons."

"Pieces of eight?" Quincy asked.

"Pieces of eight were silver," Miss Hattie Hawk said. "Do you know how they made pieces of eight? They made a bar of silver and sliced it into eight pieces."

Miss Hattie Hawk kept on looking at the coins. "Where did you find these?" she asked.

"On the beach yesterday," Quincy said. "After we got back from Azalea."

"I'll tell you where I think they came from, Quincy," said Miss Hattie Hawk. "I think they may have come from a wrecked Spanish ship."

"A galleon?" asked Quincy.

"A Spanish galleon," said Miss Hattie Hawk. "So many ships were sunk, you know. They didn't know the waters, and they had no warnings about storms, and the ships would sink. The storm may have disturbed it and washed some of its cargo toward shore."

Quincy felt a surge of excitement. "Really?" she said. "Really?"

"They've been finding lots of sunken ships over on the east coast of Florida," Miss Hattie Hawk said.

"That's fantastic," said Quincy.

"It's not fantastic at all," said Miss Hattie Hawk. "It's a matter of fact. Corporations have been formed to look for wrecks and salvage the cargo. The state has passed a new law about treasure, as a matter of fact. It's a big business over there on the east coast. Of course, the route of the Spanish ships was right over there. I don't know that many Spanish cargo vessels came up this far in the Gulf. The main route was from Veracruz to Havana and then to Spain." She got up. "Excuse me, Quincy, let me heat up the coffee."

Quincy kept on sitting there, looking out at the bay, and thinking of Spanish galleons. It was the most romantic thing she'd ever heard of in her life . . . much better than buried treasure. Was there a wrecked galleon right out there in Turtle Harbor?

Miss Hattie Hawk came back with the coffeepot and poured herself another cup. "If I were you, Quincy, I wouldn't spread it around about that gold. Treasure hunters are the worst kind of people in the world. They'd come in here to St. Jerome in hordes and overrun the place. They'd drive everybody crazy. But that's a Spanish coin, all right. There's no getting around that."

She put her cup down and said, "I'm not going to drink any more coffee. I'm going over to Arcadia Marsh to cut some cattails. Do you want to go with me?"

"What?" said Quincy, whose mind was drifting off into a dreamworld of Spanish ships laden with treasure which were sunk right in front of their house. "Oh, no, ma'am, thank you," she said when she realized what Miss Hattie Hawk had said. "But thank you for the biscuits and the information."

She left Miss Hattie Hawk's house and went and sat on the beach and thought. She had to find out more about Spanish ships and wrecked ships and treasure salvage, that was for sure. And she was not to tell anyone. That would be a switch—trying to keep people from getting interested in what she was doing instead of trying to get them interested.

She got up and started walking along the beach, eyes down, looking, searching for more coins. She would become a worse beachcomber than Mike Standish, she thought.

Ten

After supper Quincy took her telescope down to the clearing and set it up.

She brooded once more about her family. Not one of them had the slightest conception of what it meant to her, the whole world of physics and mathematics and astronomy that she lumped in her mind under the vague heading of Science. And that was an even less accurate title, she realized, since she'd met Mike Standish, whose interest was in the biological sciences, which she didn't consider part of her Science at all.

She tried to tell them sometimes what it meant to her, this conception of the world she'd stumbled on. What it meant to know that sand and seawater and seashells and twigs are all made up of neutrons and protons and electrons separated by space . . . that there are sextillion protons, neutrons, and electrons in one tiny coquina shell . . . that the whole universe is made up of tiny solar systems. . . .

Earlier, when everybody had been sitting around, Grandmama had said, "The world is divided into groups of people.

Some people can't stand the beach, period. Some people like beaches like Cape Cod or Cape May or Miami Beach. Some people like Turtle Point. And some people appreciate St. Jerome."

"Grandmama, that's like the Hertzsprung-Russell diagram," Quincy had said.

"What's that?"

"It's a graph that plots the stars," Quincy had explained. "The vertical scale measures luminosity, and the horizontal scale measures temperature. The hot bright stars are on the upper left, and the dim cool stars are on the lower right."

A stunned silence had greeted this.

"You know," Quincy had said, "the cool dim stars are people who don't like any beaches at all. The hot bright stars are people who like St. Jerome. And the Cape Codders—" She saw the grown-ups beginning to smile. "You know, stars fall into distinct groupings," she said, trying to make it clear to them. She made the mistake of mentioning the logarithmically increasing brightness, which she'd enjoyed reading about, but which she realized she didn't understand well enough to explain to anybody. "You can look it up," she said.

"I wouldn't know what kinds of books to look those things you talk about up in," Melissa had said. "And I wouldn't want to read those books anyway."

"You couldn't understand them," Quincy had said. "I predict you'll flunk math and science at Bennington."

"There are more important things on the curriculum," Melissa had said.

What creeps they all were, Quincy thought now, as she set up the telescope all by herself in the little clearing. She looked up at the sky without the telescope. According to the book, in the early evening Jupiter was supposed to be visible right over there.

Jupiter, the book had said, was the most interesting of all the planets, and Quincy could see why anybody would think so. It had a red spot near its equator, and the red spot might even be a hurricane, a hurricane that had lasted two hundred years. And you could see at least four of the moons of Jupiter with a telescope.

Quincy thought of a hurricane that lasted two hundred years, and she shivered.

Okay, that was Jupiter, up there. She could see it plainly with her naked eye. Now to get the scope trained on it. She loosened the clamps and moved the tube until Jupiter was in the scope's cross hairs.

She clamped it and brought the eyepiece into focus. The telescope was still a little confusing to her because it inverted everything.

But there was Jupiter, as clear and sharp and bright as it could be.

And there were the moons.

Four little moons in a row, two on either side of Jupiter.

She moved her head and looked at Jupiter without the scope. No moons. She looked in the telescope again, and there they were!

Her heart pounded, and she wanted to shout. She did shout. "I found it! I found it!" she shouted.

She ran back to her house, but nobody was there. Oh, they'd all gone down to the Motts' for popsicles. She raced down to the Motts'.

"I found it!" she shouted. "I found it. Come look at Jupiter!"

"Jupiter?" everyone said.

Oh, what dullards they were, Quincy thought. What idiots.

"Come and see Jupiter and its moons in the telescope," she said. "They're strung out like little beads. Molly. Mama. Jill. Papa. Grandmama. Somebody, come."

"I'll come," Mrs. Luckie said. She took Mr. Luckie's hand, and Mr. Luckie said, "I'll come, too."

Jill got up, and Quincy's grandparents, and finally everybody trailed down to the telescope.

Quincy adjusted it for her mother first, and her mother looked—and squealed with delight. "Ooooh! They're beautiful!" she said.

"I know," Quincy said. "Galileo freaked out when he saw them, too."

She adjusted the telescope for her father.

"Galileo kept looking at them, and he saw how they moved," she said.

She adjusted the scope for Sam.

"He had a telescope smaller than mine, too," she said.

It was one of the proudest moments of Quincy's life. She was very happy—and everybody praised her for finding Jupiter and thanked her for showing it to them. Then they all filtered back to the Motts' house. All except Molly, who sat on the top of the steps going down to the beach with Quincy.

"How did you ever get interested in all this?" Molly asked her.

"I don't know," said Quincy. "I guess I always have been interested and didn't know it. Then when I started school and learned to read, I read all the books in the school library. I mean, I read all the story books, the fiction. So I started on the next section, and those were the science books. And I read a book about astronomy. It had pictures of stars and planets. There was a big full-page picture of the moon. I felt like it was my moon. The picture was so big and so bright that it almost scared me. Well, not really scared me, but you know, it hit me in the stomach."

"I know," Molly said. "Like a fast elevator going down."

"That's right. And then I read some of the other books on science, and I found out that the whole world is made up of little solar systems. I was thinking about that tonight. Atoms have neutrons and protons revolving like planets around the sun. I couldn't believe it when I read it—and yet I knew it was the truest thing I'd ever heard. After that, plays and stories and music—well, they were all right if I had nothing better to do, but I had something better to do."

"Did living in Houston with the space program and all— I thought maybe that was the reason," Molly said.

"Not really. I just watched it on television like you did. But I do remember the first man on the moon. It was July 20, 1969, and Neil Armstrong and Buzz Aldrin landed on the moon, my moon. And the first words they said were 'Houston, the Eagle has landed.' I remember that. And they walked on the moon."

The girls sat on the top step, hugging their knees.

"And my family simply does not understand," Quincy said. "My mother tries. She really does. But her mind is so much on plays and books and stuff like that she can't understand that anybody who lives near her is interested in something she doesn't know anything about.

"I said I wanted a chemistry set for Christmas last year, and they said I was too old. I was eleven. They thought a chemistry set was a toy. I wanted one so I could get used to handling the equipment and doing experiments. I didn't want it to play with at all. But I couldn't make them understand.

"My mother sees that we have tickets to every play in Houston and every ballet and lots of concerts. But she never remembers that I like to see the shows at the planetarium. She's not *mean* about it, but she doesn't remember. I just started going to the planetarium by myself."

Quincy sighed. She felt sad, now that she'd poured all this out to Molly Mott. Especially after everybody had been so nice about Jupiter. Oh, well.

"Parents," said Molly, "are a shuck."

Molly was lazy, thought Quincy, but she had a gift for the telling phrase.

Eleven

Melissa came home from work early one day—riding on the back of a motorcycle.

The driver of the motorcycle was named Dallas Truitt. He worked in the marina on Turtle Point, and he'd stopped in the Shell Shop that afternoon and had seen Melissa.

When she found out she was getting off earlier than she'd expected and realized she needed a ride to St. Jerome, Dallas offered to bring her.

"I just happened to have an extra helmet," he said.

And so Melissa had climbed on the back of the motorcycle and had ridden home in splendor, arriving behind the Luckie house with a great deal of noise and dust.

Everybody came out to meet Dallas and look at the motorcycle.

Quincy decided immediately that Dallas was the most interesting boy Melissa had ever brought home. All of her boyfriends in Houston had been like Luckies themselves— good students, talented, leaders, talkers. Quincy had disliked them all, especially the ones who were president of the

Key Club or president of the senior class or president of the dramatic club. They were just more people who were busy and bright and not interested in anything she had to say.

But Dallas seemed different. He wasn't handsome, but he was tanned and looked strong and he seemed at ease with himself and with his motorcycle.

When he saw how interested everybody was in his motorcycle, he offered to take everybody for rides. He took Jill for a short ride down the dirt road through the Jungle, and then he took the cycle down on the beach where it was more fun to ride. He took Sam and then Quincy.

Quincy loved it. She clutched Dallas around the waist and peered out from under the edge of the helmet at the bluff on one side and the water on the other, both racing past, it seemed. She loved the wind on her face and the speed. She almost loved Dallas.

When they stopped in front of the steps, Dallas turned around and looked at her as she climbed off. "You really liked it, didn't you?" he said. "I could tell."

Quincy was somehow pleased, as though he were praising her.

"Ducky loves all motors," Melissa said. "She even wants a motorboat instead of a sailboat."

"What's wrong with that?" Quincy asked.

"Sails are quieter and more natural," Melissa said. "Sailing is organic. It doesn't use energy."

"Motors get you there," said Dallas.

"Sometimes they do," said Mrs. Luckie. "Sometimes motors conk out, too. Just like the wind."

"Don't you want to come for a ride?" Dallas said to Mrs. Luckie.

To everyone's astonishment, Mrs. Luckie said she'd like to try it. She put on the helmet and climbed on the motorcycle, and Dallas took off in a great clatter and rush. When they got back, Mrs. Luckie looked a little dazed but said that she was glad she'd tried it.

"It's bouncy, like riding a horse," she said, "but lots noisier."

The grandparents had come down to watch the fun and Dallas almost persuaded Mrs. Ballew to go for a ride, but she finally decided not to try it.

Mr. Luckie said he had to start supper. He invited Dallas to stay, and Dallas accepted.

"Do we have time for a swim?" Melissa asked.

"Sure," said Mr. Luckie.

"And sailing?" Jill asked. "Let's take Dallas for a sail."

"Great!" said Dallas, and Melissa, Quincy was happy to see, looked a little cross that everybody was enjoying her new young man so much.

Then one of those great afternoons at St. Jerome took place that made it so hard for everybody to understand why Quincy would want to spend a summer anywhere but there.

The tide was high and the swimming was good. People took turns sailing, and those who weren't sailing dived off the float that somebody had rigged up out of oil drums to replace the dock.

All the young people at St. Jerome came down to join in—Molly and her little brother and the kids from way down at the end and the Caldwells and the Dukes. Mike Standish came down to the beach carrying a bucket and wearing a shirt and shorts. He stopped and solemnly watched the crowd for a while, and then he disappeared, returning in a little while in a bathing suit.

He didn't seem very much at home in the water, Quincy thought. He waded out and began to swim a little, in a stiff, swimming-class sort of style.

Mrs. Standish came down with Petey, her little old terrier, and set up a folding chair on the beach and began to shell butter beans and keep an eye on things. Mrs. Ballew brought her knitting down.

There was much splashing and laughter, but Quincy noticed that Molly didn't go in swimming. She sat with the grandmothers, and after a while Mike walked over and sat down with them.

Dallas went sailing with Melissa and Jill, and Quincy watched him bringing the boat back to shore. He looked very capable and confident, holding the tiller and sheet, watching the wake.

Jill called to Mike and asked him if he'd like to go for a sail, and Mike hesitated.

"Go on, Michael," Mrs. Standish said. "Your father was a great sailor when he was your age."

Mike got up and went out with Sam and Jill. Quincy, in the water, watched the little boat sail out into the harbor and come about, heading toward the beach.

Mike had the tiller, and as the boat came closer, Quincy could see him sitting ramrod-stiff, staring straight ahead. All went well until the boat got near the float and the swimmers. Suddenly, it capsized.

Everybody helped get the boat upright again—it was easy in the shallow water.

"Don't worry, Mike," said Jill. "When we had a Sunfish, we used to take it out into the bay and turn it over on purpose. It was so easy to get it up again—you just stepped on the centerboard—and we loved to turn it over and duck everybody."

Mike was obviously embarrassed, even though everybody was being nice about it. He left, saying he wanted to go put on his clothes.

Quincy dropped down on the sand beside Molly.

"I feel sorry for Mike," Quincy said.

"Me, too," Molly said, "except he can look so funny sometimes. When he got all wet, he looked like one of his sea creatures."

"He doesn't seem to get very tan," Quincy said. "But why do you suppose he can't swim better? Don't people learn how to swim in New York?"

"Maybe he knows too much about what's in the water," Molly said.

Nearly everybody at St. Jerome came to the Luckies' house for supper that night. Mr. Ballew had caught mullet with his cast net, and Mr. Luckie had cooked them. (They had shared the cleaning of the mullet.)

Mike Standish had never eaten mullet before.

"We don't eat it in the East," he explained.

"Oh, that's a different kind of mullet," said Mr. Luckie. "You only catch this good kind of mullet from Cedar Key, Florida, around the Gulf Coast to Louisiana. Craig Claiborne had a column about mullet in the *New York Times* one time."

"Oh, well, if it was in the *New York Times*," said Mike. And he took a piece of mullet.

Dallas, it turned out, was in college at Florida State University.

"What are you studying?" Mrs. Luckie asked. "Their drama department is great."

"I'm majoring in physics," Dallas said. "I want to go into astrophysics."

71

You could almost hear the clicks of minds closing as the Luckies all lost interest in Dallas's schooling.

"Oh," said Mrs. Luckie faintly. "How interesting."

"It *is* interesting," said Quincy. "FSU is where they discovered ten new elements."

"That's right, and one of those men is my adviser," Dallas said.

Quincy was awestruck. Here was somebody—the first person she'd ever met—who not only had had courses in physics but liked them. And moreover, he knew some really first-rate scientists. She couldn't stop staring at Dallas.

She had known right away he was different. He was not only the nicest boy Melissa had ever brought home, but the kind of person she had always wanted to meet.

Dallas noticed her staring at him and smiled at her.

"I like physics, too," she said softly, but he didn't hear her.

After supper everybody went down on the beach to watch the sunset, except Mr. Luckie, who stayed home to make some ice cream.

The tide was low and there was a great expanse of sand to walk on. The sun was red and the sky was a pearly pink. Petey ran across the damp sand chasing terns whenever one would land.

"Petey helps the fish," said Quincy.

When Mr. Luckie called, they all trooped back to the house and sat on the front porch, eating ice cream and talking.

"This is a sensual delight," Melissa said. "The beach, ice cream, the sunset. . . ."

And they all began to talk about the same old things— how wonderful St. Jerome was and how Turtle Point had been practically wiped out, just as they had always known it would be. They began to laugh about the dock being gone and the trouble the dock committee was having getting anything done . . . and then they laughed about Mike capsizing the boat on top of the swimmers.

And because they didn't mean to be unkind, they quickly assured Mike it hadn't been bad . . . that they'd all done things that were just as inept.

"What does inept mean?" Molly's little brother asked.

"Stupid," said Molly.

"I am not!" Pennington shouted angrily.

Everybody laughed again.

"Do you remember that time we went sailing with Charlie Standish and that other boy?" Mrs. Luckie said to Mrs. Mott. "We went out in that big boat the Standishes used to have, and we were out in the Gulf. And the boat turned over. We didn't know what to do, so Charlie said he'd swim in to get help. He left the three of us hanging onto that boat and he swam to Turtle Point and walked across the Point and then he swam across Turtle Harbor to St. Jerome. He got to his house, and his mother was sitting on the front porch shelling peas. And do you know what Charlie Standish did? He walked right past her without a word and went inside and took a shower before he told her or anybody else what had happened! None of us ever got over that! There we were, out in the Gulf of Mexico, and Charlie takes a shower before he gets any help!"

It was a familiar story, and everybody laughed at it again.

"He didn't say one word to me," Mrs. Standish said. "He walked right past me, and when he took his shower he came back and said, 'Ma, we've got to go get help. . . .' "

Everybody laughed once more, and somebody said, "I bet

73

it wasn't so funny at the time," and Mrs. Luckie said, "It certainly wasn't."

"Listen, now's a good time to talk about the Summer Show," Jill said.

"Oh, for heaven's sake," said Quincy.

Everybody had to explain the Summer Show to Dallas, who was impressed.

"Where do you put it on?" he asked.

"In the pavilion," Melissa explained. "That big screened building back of the houses."

"Was the pavilion built for the Summer Show?" Quincy asked.

"Heavens, no," said Mrs. Luckie. "It was there when I was a little girl."

"We built it for fish fries and sociables," Mr. Ballew explained. "It's going to fall down, too, if we don't look out. Everybody at St. Jerome used to help keep it up, but nobody cares anymore. It's on our lot so I guess it's our responsibility. Well, that's not right—because you certainly help," he said, turning to Mr. Standish.

"Anyway, it's not a first-class theater, but it'll do," Melissa said.

"One year we had the Show on the dock and had a water ballet," Jill said.

"That was the worst show," Quincy said, "the worst show ever."

"But that awful woman was staying here with the Caldwells," Mrs. Luckie said, "and she wanted to teach all the girls precision swimming."

"It was ghastly," said Quincy.

"Molly hasn't been in the water since," Mrs. Mott said. "It might have been good if all you girls had cooperated. . . ."

"But we didn't want to cooperate," Quincy said. "Why is it that when grown-ups talk about kids cooperating it always means kids doing something kids don't want to do?"

Silence met this question. Until Mr. Luckie spoke. "Cooperation means everybody giving in a little for the common good."

"But what was she giving in?" Quincy asked. "Oh, forget it!"

"Back to this year's Show," Mrs. Luckie said. "Do you really want to write it ourselves?"

"Yes!"

"Yes!"

Quincy and Molly did not join in the chorus.

"I hope you're not biting off more than you can chew," Mr. Luckie said.

"We can do it," said Jill. "It will be super."

"Even if we don't write our own music, we can write new words to old songs and use them," Mrs. Luckie said.

"It will work," Jill said.

"Let's go," Quincy hissed to Molly. "Come on."

They picked up her telescope and took it to the clearing and set it up.

That was the night Quincy first saw Saturn through the telescope.

Even Molly was impressed. "It looks great," she said. "Like the pictures on calendars or something. . . . What is it? Tire advertisements?"

"Only it's better," Quincy said, "since it's the real thing."

"Are you going to call the others?" Molly asked her.

"Oh, why bother?" Quincy said. "They're talking about that dumb old Show."

She knelt down and looked again at Saturn, with its rings. How could anybody be more interested in the Show than in the planets? Of course, they'd want to see Saturn, she thought. "Let's go get them," she said to Molly.

As they got closer to the Luckies' house, they could hear everybody laughing. Then somebody said something and they all laughed again.

"They're having a great time," Molly said.

"That's because they're being so creative," Quincy said, and she and Molly began to laugh as hard as the people on the porch.

As the girls came up the porch steps, there was a brief lull in the talk and laughter, and then somebody said, "And then we could have Miss Hattie Hawk with her binoculars and her khaki pants—" Laughter interrupted the speaker.

There didn't seem to be much point in asking if anybody wanted to see Saturn, but then you never knew, Quincy decided.

"Does anybody want to see Saturn? And its rings?" Quincy asked when the laughter died down. "I've found Saturn."

"Was it lost?" asked Mr. Standish, and everybody laughed again.

"I'll come, Ducky," Mrs. Luckie said.

My mother does try, thought Quincy.

In the end, nearly everybody trooped down to the telescope, and they stooped or knelt and Quincy kept adjusting the telescope, and they all said how bright it was and how unusual it looked, and the grandparents said Ducky was so smart to find Saturn with a telescope.

And then everybody left.

"Where's your boyfriend?" Quincy asked Melissa.

"Oh, he had to leave," Melissa said.

Quincy was fiercely disappointed. She wanted Dallas to

know she, too, was interested in astronomy, and she wanted to talk to him about it. She had a million questions to ask somebody like Dallas. And he'd left.

"Got tired of you, did he?" she asked Melissa.

Melissa tossed her long black hair back. "Hardly," she said. "If anybody's tired of anybody, I'm tired of him."

Melissa had no sense at all, Quincy thought. She preferred those dumb boys she went out with in Houston, preferred them to a neat person like Dallas, who had a motorcycle and studied physics.

Twelve

So Quincy's days took on a kind of pattern. At night, when it was clear, she used her telescope.

During the day, she checked on LeMoyne, watched her grandfather pull in the shark line, chatted with her grandmother, fished, talked to Molly, and checked the crab traps.

After the dock was washed away, the Ballews and the Luckies started tying their crab traps to empty bleach bottles, which acted as markers, floating and bobbing on the surface of Turtle Harbor.

And she beachcombed. She walked the beach, head down, scuffing the sand, watching for the glint of gold. Several times at low tide, she found more gold coins.

Finally, she resolved to do something, to find out somehow if it were possible that there was a wrecked Spanish galleon out there in Turtle Harbor.

I need books, she told herself. I've got to get to the library.

Getting to the library was enormously difficult. There was no library in Elysium; the closest one was in Azalea, forty miles away.

And nobody seemed to be going to Azalea any time soon. At least not in my lifetime, Quincy thought sourly.

She kept asking, with no luck.

"What about the dock committee?" she asked her father. "Won't they have to go to Azalea?"

"No, they've agreed to let Mr. Bite in Elysium do the work," her father said. "But he's got so much work to do on Turtle Point and at St. Lucy—on account of the hurricane damage—that he won't get to our dock for a while. That will give the committee longer to discuss things." Mr. Luckie sounded depressed.

"I miss the dock. Wouldn't it be quicker to go get somebody in Azalea?" Quincy asked.

"Oh, no," said Mr. Luckie. "It would take *years* to decide who to talk to in Azalea."

"Have you read all those books you checked out when we were in town during the hurricane?" her mother asked her.

"Long ago," said Quincy. "Even the one about quasars."

Finally, Quincy thought of a way to get action. She said to her grandmother, "You know when we went into Azalea for the storm, I checked out those books on your card at the library. . . . I really ought to take them back."

Grandmama was a stickler for doing things when you should. She didn't believe in overparking or overdue books at the library either. She said she'd just go into town herself and take those books back.

"But I want to check out some more books," Quincy said. "Can't I go with you?"

"That would mean I'd have to take you back in two weeks—or four weeks, I guess it is—to return those books," Grandmama said. "Let me think about it."

Then Dallas Truitt, who always seemed to be around the

house these days, offered to take Quincy to Azalea on the back of his motorcycle.

Quincy could think of no better way to get to Azalea.

But Mrs. Luckie refused to allow it. "It's too far," she said. "Forty miles is too far for you to ride on a motorcycle. And forty miles back. No."

"I don't mind," Quincy said.

"No."

"Too bad," said Dallas. "We would have had a trip."

"Dallas, there's something I want to ask you."

"What?"

"You know quasars?" Quincy said.

"I know what they are, yes," Dallas said.

"Well, I've been reading this book about quasars, and it says they exhibit a red shift of extreme magnitude in their spectrums. Some as great as two hundred percent. This book says that this may mean that the quasar is receding at a rapid rate. . . ."

Everyone but Dallas began to laugh at Quincy, but Dallas was listening intently and seriously, and Quincy plowed on. "Anyway, the book says that the energy produced by the quasars must be tremendous because they're so far away. I read somewhere else that neutron stars are very dense, many thousands of pounds per inch. Isn't that enough to slow light down? So my question is, could quasars be very dense and could they rob the light escaping from them of energy and wouldn't that account for their red shift?"

"Hmmm," said Dallas. "One argument against that theory is that if the quasars are nearby and massive, why don't we see the effects of their gravity? The gravitational red shift is an accepted feature of general relativity. . . ."

Quincy listened intently. Her mother and Melissa and

her grandmother began to chatter about the weather and the Summer Show, but Dallas went on to list the arguments in favor of quasars being a type of galaxy—their radio emissions and their spectra—and offered a compromise argument that the red shift might be partly due to "Doppler shift."

Quincy hated for the talk to end. She stretched it out as long as she could with as many questions as she could muster. And Dallas answered all of them with utmost patience as well as he could.

At last, though, he wrote down for her the name of a fundamental book on astronomy and handed it to her, and then—as Quincy had known he would—he got up and moved over by Melissa.

In the end, Mrs. Ballew drove Quincy to Azalea the next week.

At the library, Quincy found a very good book about salvaging wrecks off the Florida east coast. She leaned against the bookshelves and looked through it. At first it looked a bit daunting, with its pictures of divers with tanks of oxygen on their backs, the divers hacking away at anchors crusted with corrosion and coral . . . and its maps showing locations of known wrecked ships. But there were some useful bits, including the story of how one man located a wrecked ship by paddling around on an inner tube in the area where he thought a ship had gone down and peering down through a snorkeling mask.

Scuba diving might be impossible, at least for now, but snorkeling was very easy. Quincy shut the book and started toward the circulation desk. Then she decided to go see if she could find some more Arthur C. Clarke books she hadn't read, to check the astronomy shelf, and maybe something else. She was in luck. She found two more Clarkes and a book on the Messier objects in the sky.

She began to read the book on the Messier objects on the way back to the beach.

"Did you know," she asked her grandmother, "that a Frenchman named Messier cataloged lots of the nebulae in the sky? And that he didn't catalog them because he was interested in nebulae, but because he was looking for comets? He just wanted to list all the small hazy things that looked like comets and weren't. Isn't that amazing?"

"It truly is," said her grandmother.

Quincy read on. "If you can find and identify all of the 103 Messier objects," said the book, "you are no longer a beginner in stargazing."

That was a worthy goal, thought Quincy.

When she and her grandmother got home, she settled down in the hammock on her front porch to read the book on treasure ships. She skimmed the parts about the information from the Archives of the Indies in Seville, Spain, about galleons that had sunk on their way back to Spain with treasure from the New World.

The main route of the galleons had been far away from Turtle Harbor, but then there were documented cases of ships that had strayed off course and sunk.

A number of things were fascinating. One, of course, was the man who paddled around on his inner tube until he located a wreck. Another was the fact that Spanish ships had often carried porcelain from China which had been shipped to Mexico, hauled overland to the Gulf, and then loaded on ships for Spain. Photographs of the porcelain showed it to be all blue and white.

I knew there was something about that broken piece of

blue-and-white china! Quincy said to herself. I knew it! There were pictures of gold coins like hers in the book, and pictures of silver coins. Silver coins were usually covered with a thick green crust, she learned. She closed her eyes and tried to remember if she'd seen any green, crusty things lying on the beach. She was sure she had.

She hid the book on salvage under her telescope and started down to the beach to see what else she could find, but at the edge of the bluff she realized it was high tide and beachcombing would be no good. She could do it later.

She sat on the steps and thought about how to look for a wreck. She needed help, she decided.

She couldn't go on an inner tube, not out in the harbor all by herself. If she had help, she could go out in the sailboat and then look. She could rightfully claim the Luckies' sailboat every third day. Usually, Sam and Jill shared it, each taking it on alternate days. She had never demanded a fair share of the boat's time because she hadn't cared that much about sailing, but now that she needed a boat, she would ask for her share.

But she needed help. It would be asinine to go out in the boat by herself. Who would help?

She thought of all the people at St. Jerome. Her parents. Sam. Jill. She rejected them all. For one thing, they'd probably be as disinterested in Spanish treasure, if she told them about it, as they were in astronomy. For another thing, her father was busy with the dock committee and cooking, and her mother and Jill and Sam were busy with the Summer Show.

Her grandfather had a motorboat, and he liked to go out in it—but he liked to fish. Miss Hattie Hawk? Quincy gave a good bit of thought to Miss Hattie Hawk as a co-conspirator and colleague, but in the end she decided she was too much in awe of Miss Hattie Hawk to invite her to come and help her find a sunken Spanish galleon with an inner tube and a snorkel mask.

The Caldwell children and the Duke boys were too young. She lumped all the people down at the end of the bluff in one vague bundle and realized she didn't know any of them well enough to ask them to help.

That left Molly Mott and Mike Standish.

What a pair, she thought.

But they were all she had, she decided. Molly was downright lazy, but she was an awfully good-tempered girl. She was sure to help if Quincy asked her to.

And Mike, well, Mike was still something of an unknown quantity. But he had brains, there was no denying that. He was kind of a loner, always off beachcombing, but then he seemed anxious in a way to fit into things at St. Jerome, to belong, so maybe he'd go along.

She would ask them.

Simple greed was on her side.

For who could resist the lure of Spanish treasure?

Thirteen

Molly Mott could resist the lure of Spanish gold.

"I don't believe it," she said when Quincy told her what she wanted.

Quincy showed her the coins and told her what Miss Hattie Hawk had said, showed her the library book.

"I don't believe there's any treasure ship out there," Molly said. "And if there is one, I don't want to help you look for it."

"You wouldn't have to get out of the boat," Quincy said. "You could just sit there."

"I'd get sunburned," Molly said.

"You ought to get in the sun more," Quincy said. "You're so white now you glow in the dark."

Molly said nothing. She just sat there. Quincy gave up. She realized that bigger, louder, more powerful people than she had given up yelling at Molly to do something she didn't want to do.

Quincy stamped off to find Mike Standish.

She found him, as usual, on the beach. He had been down

to Sting Ray Point, he said, looking for more sea cucumbers in the grass down there.

Mike was considerably tanner than he had been. At least he stays out in the sun a lot, Quincy said to herself.

"You remember that gold thing I found on the beach after the storm?" she asked him. "It was Spanish gold."

"How do you know?" asked Mike.

"Miss Hattie Hawk said it was."

"How does she know?"

How could anyone doubt the authority of Miss Hattie Hawk? Quincy wondered. But Mike was from New York and didn't really understand that when Miss Hattie Hawk said she knew something she knew it. She described Miss Hattie Hawk's credentials.

"And I saw pictures in a book," Quincy said.

"Let me see the book," Mike said.

"Don't you believe me?" Quincy asked.

"I have a certain amount of scientific skepticism," Mike said. "Let's see the book."

"I have to go to the house to get it," Quincy said.

"I'll go with you," Mike said.

"I hid it," Quincy said. "I'll go get it."

"Why did you hide it?"

"Miss Hattie Hawk said not to let anybody know about the Spanish gold," Quincy said.

"Where did the gold come from?" Mike said.

"I think it's from a sunken galleon offshore somewhere," Quincy said. "The hurricane must have dislodged some of it, and coins have been washing ashore ever since."

"That's fantastic," Mike said.

"Miss Hattie Hawk would say it wasn't fantastic at all, but a matter of fact," Quincy said.

"I have scientific skepticism," Mike said again.

"I'll go get the book," Quincy aid. "Wait on the steps."

When she came back with the book, Mike took it and began to read it. He was fascinated, Quincy could see.

"Will you help me look for the sunken ship?" Quincy said.

"How?"

"It shows you in here," Quincy said, taking the book to find the pictures of the man who located the wreck with a snorkel mask.

"We can't do deep-sea diving," Mike said. "Or hire divers."

"No, no," said Quincy. "This man paddled around on an inner tube with just a snorkel mask. We can take our sailboat out into the harbor and get out and paddle around and look on the bottom. . . ."

"Can you sail it?"

"Of course," Quincy said.

"I guess it's worth a try," Mike said. "Even if it is fantastic."

"Everything good is fantastic," said Quincy.

They began to make definite plans.

"I can get the boat every third day—maybe more often since Sam and Jill are busy with the Summer Show. We can go out there and look and see what we can find," Quincy said.

"I'm not a good swimmer," Mike said.

"You could stay in the boat while I paddle around on an inner tube or a float," Quincy said.

"I don't know," Mike said.

"You *can* swim, can't you?" Quincy asked.

"I had swimming lessons," Mike said. "Once. But I'm not

a good swimmer like everybody else down here."

Quincy had never met anybody as old as Mike who wasn't a good swimmer. She didn't know what to say.

"But I'll try it," he said.

"Okay," said Quincy. "I'm trying to get Molly Mott to go with us. If she goes, she can stay in the boat and you can paddle around with me. If she won't go, you can stay in the boat."

"If she goes, she'd be a third person to divide the treasure with," Mike said.

"True," said Quincy, thinking that Mike was very practical and also very optimistic about finding treasure. "But it would be kind of nice if Molly went with us."

"Why?" asked Mike.

"Oh, just because," said Quincy. What she was thinking about was that everybody would start teasing her about Mike being her boyfriend if they went out in the sailboat every third day. And what a pain that would be! She'd have to make Molly go, that was all there was to it.

Mike said he'd like to take the library book home with him so he could study it, and Quincy said that was all right. "But don't let your grandparents see it," she said.

"Somehow I can't see my grandfather trying to muscle in on my treasure trove," said Mike.

"I guess not," Quincy said. "But just the same . . . don't tell anybody."

Quincy went by the Motts' house to invite Molly to lunch.

"It's crab cakes," Quincy said. "We finally caught enough crabs at one time."

"I don't like crab," Molly said.

"The crabs are all cleaned, Molly," Quincy said. "My

father sat out on the porch this morning and cleaned them."

"Okay," Molly said. "I'll come."

As they walked toward Quincy's house, Molly said, "You know, your father is an awfully patient person when he's doing things that take a lot of time, isn't he? He'll chop things up for salads and he'll take time to fry a lot of things."

"He's patient where food is concerned," Quincy said.

"That's wonderful," Molly said. "My mother never cooks anything but roasts."

"Papa *is* a good cook," Quincy conceded.

At lunch, Quincy asked if she could use the sailboat the next day.

Everybody looked surprised. "What do you want it for?" Sam asked. "To look at stars?"

"I want to use it," Quincy said.

"You haven't used it all summer, have you?" Mrs. Luckie said. "Sure, you can use it. You hadn't planned anything special tomorrow, had you?" She looked at Sam and at Jill. Both shook their heads.

"That's settled," Quincy said.

Molly was looking at Mr. Luckie with her enormous blue eyes. "Why do you do all the cooking?" she asked him.

Everybody laughed.

"It's because the way my mother cooks is to put a pot on the stove and go do something else until she smells it burning," Sam said.

Mrs. Luckie was laughing along with everybody else. "That's right," she said. "I'm not a good cook. Oh, I used to try, but I got tired of it after about twenty-five years. I just got so I couldn't stand to cook."

"She cooked for the first twenty-five years," Mr. Luckie said. "I'll cook for the next twenty-five years. Then it's her turn again."

"Mama, you're a good cook," Sam said. "When you pay attention. But you just don't pay attention."

"I guess not," Mrs. Luckie said. "Sometimes I wonder if I do anything really well."

It always astonished Quincy when grown-ups expressed doubts about themselves.

"I tell you something you do really well," Sam said.

"What?" asked Mrs. Luckie.

"Float," said Sam.

Everybody laughed and agreed that Mrs. Luckie was the champion floater of Turtle Harbor.

After lunch, Quincy and Molly sat in the hammock while everybody went off to take naps.

"Molly, you've got to go with me in the boat tomorrow. Mike Standish is going, and if we go by ourselves everybody will tease me. You know how it will be," Quincy said.

"Oh, all right," Molly said. "But you have to do something for me sometime. And promise me I don't have to get out of the boat."

"Sure," said Quincy.

Fourteen

The next day Molly and Mike met Quincy at the Luckies' house at nine o'clock. Under Quincy's direction they gathered up masks and snorkels, an inner tube and a float, flippers, an ice chest and some cold drinks, sandwiches and potato chips.

"Here, get the life jackets," Quincy said.

"Oh, we won't need them," Molly said. "We can't carry all this."

"It's a rule," Quincy said. "I won't be allowed to use the boat if we go off without them."

"Oh, all right," Molly said. They carried the gear down to the beach where the Luckies' boat was pulled up, dumped the stuff aboard, pushed the boat out a little way, and clambered in.

"Oh, we forgot the paddles," said Quincy.

"Why don't you leave them in the boat like everybody else?" Molly asked.

"I don't know," Quincy said. "Some people take them up." She got out of the boat. "Come on, Molly, let's go get them. Toss out the anchor, Mike."

"This is the silliest thing I ever heard of," Molly said, as they climbed the steps from the beach. "We'll never find a wrecked galleon."

"You may be right," Quincy said. "But it's like Everest. It's here."

"We don't know that it's here," Molly said.

"I mean the search is here," said Quincy. "The quest. We have to look."

When they arrived back at the beach, Mike got out and said he'd push the boat out farther if the girls would get in. Quincy sat with the tiller in hand. Molly even stirred herself to pull in the anchor, and Mike pushed the boat and then climbed in himself.

"You're learning about boats," Quincy said.

Mike smiled gratefully, and Quincy realized it was the first time she'd seen him smile.

"I wish I knew more about boats," he said.

"I'll be glad to teach you all I know," Quincy said.

She turned the tiller so the boat swung about and the sail caught the wind, and the boat moved swiftly down the harbor along the shoreline.

"We really want to go straight out," Quincy said, "but the wind's offshore, so we'll go down this way a little bit and then head back down."

"That's called tacking," Mike said. "I read it in a book."

Quincy said nothing for a few minutes. It was a new sensation to be the most experienced sailor in the boat—and not a particularly pleasant one, to get right down to it. She wasn't all that confident. This boat was bigger than the Sunfish in which she'd learned to sail, and it was harder to handle. It was a whole lot more serious if it went over. She'd have to be careful not to come about too suddenly, be careful to come about into the wind, be careful not to jibe, be careful not to get exactly before the wind so they went too fast. . . . She tried to remember everything she had to be careful of and wished she had gotten more sailing experience, but then Sam or Jill had always been out in the boat.

"Coming about!" she said, and they all ducked as the boom swung over, and they came about neatly and headed back toward the mouth of Turtle Harbor.

Mike and Molly shifted sides.

Quincy felt a tremendous surge of relief. She had managed that all right, hadn't she? She could sail, couldn't she, as long as the wind didn't get any stronger . . . and as long as the wind blew at all? Right now, she had to admit she feared strong winds more than she feared being becalmed.

"This is kind of nice, isn't it?" Molly said, leaning back against the side of the boat and looking at the shore.

"I know," Quincy said. "Everything on shore always looks so different when you see it from way out here. The houses look so much more substantial, don't they? Different from the way they look when you're on land by them."

They looked at the houses of St. Jerome as they glided majestically down Turtle Harbor. The beach was empty— except for Grandpapa, who was out hauling in his shark line.

"Let's anchor here," said Quincy as soon as they were out in the deep water of the channel.

Mike dropped the anchor into the channel, but the rope wasn't long enough for the anchor to reach the bottom.

"I was afraid of that," Quincy said. "Let's paddle over to the edge of the channel and anchor it on that bank."

This worked. The little boat headed into the wind, and its sail drooped. The anchor rope held.

"Now we can get out," Quincy said. "Put on your life jackets."

"I'm not going to get out of the boat," Molly said.

"Okay," said Quincy. "You stay in, and you can paddle the boat and follow us while we look."

Mike had finished buckling his life jacket, and he sat there in the bottom of the boat.

"Now we look for piles of ballast rock or big old anchors and things like that," Mike said. "Not the hulls of ships . . . the book says the wood rots."

"That's right," Quincy said.

She checked her life jacket and put on a mask. She picked up the inner tube and jumped into the channel. As she went under, she thought of all those sand sharks down on the bottom of the channel. Maybe Molly was smarter than she was. I hope those sharks just stay on the bottom, she thought, as she popped to the top of the water, inner tube in hand.

She wiggled on top of the inner tube and lay across it on her stomach. She put her head down and peered into the water.

Mike was getting ready to jump overboard. He had his float in hand, and his mask was on. "Can you see anything?" he asked.

"Nothing but weeds," said Quincy. "But I think it's clear enough to see—if there's anything to see."

They stayed out for a while, paddling about on top of the water, peering into the depths. As they moved up the channel, Molly would haul up the anchor and paddle after them to keep the boat nearby.

Occasionally, mullet jumped near them. Molly screamed when a giant ray jumped.

There were lots of little fish swimming around them and an occasional jellyfish, but nothing lethal, according to Mike.

Mike seemed more at ease now that he had found he could paddle about on the float.

Once they climbed back in the boat and everybody had a sandwich and a soda.

Some time after the break, Molly began to complain of the heat, and Quincy and Mike felt pretty baked-out, too.

"I guess we'd better go in," Quincy said. She was a little nervous when she thought about sailing them back in.

But that was easy. The wind was still offshore and had died down to where it was a nice, caressing, gentle breeze. They floated into shore and beached the boat.

"You're a great sailor," Molly said.

"Thanks," said Quincy, "but I'm not really."

"You're better than I am," Mike said.

When Quincy got home, she found it was only eleven o'clock. Good heavens! She had thought it was the middle of the afternoon. Paddling in Turtle Harbor under the Florida sun was hot work.

She took a shower and collapsed in the hammock on the front porch.

"Are you through with the boat?" Sam asked her. "For today?"

"You bet," Quincy said.

Fifteen

Two days later they went out again. Then the three of them began to spend a lot of time on the water. They took the sailboat out as often as Quincy could claim it—when the weather was fair.

When it rained, or when Quincy had to yield the boat to Sam or Jill, Quincy read Arthur C. Clarke or the book on nebulae.

But more than half the time, it seemed, they were out in the boat.

"I told you if you'd just try, if you'd just enter into things," said Mrs. Luckie, "you could have a good time at St. Jerome. And I was right. And besides, you and Molly are so good for Mike. He was out of everything for a while —Mama and Mrs. Standish were terribly worried about him —and he needed friends. I'm really proud of you and Molly, Quincy."

Quincy accepted this praise in silence. She knew quite well she hadn't "tried to enter into things" at St. Jerome, that she'd just drifted, so to speak, into treasure hunting.

Treasure hunting was a last resort. Given a choice, she'd still rather be in Houston going to Rice's summer school for high school students. It was on the tip of her tongue to tell her mother all this, but, out of long habit, she kept quiet. Either her family would laugh at the idea of treasure hunting or they'd enthusiastically take over the project and run it themselves. She'd just wait a little, she thought, to talk about it.

During those long hours in the boat, when Quincy and Mike weren't actually paddling about peering down into the dark reaches of Turtle Harbor, they talked.

Mike told them about his life in New York and how he went to private school, but now that his mother was separated from his father he would have to go to public school, and he dreaded it. He told them how he rode the buses and subways all over Manhattan and went to the Museum of Natural History for classes every Saturday. He told them about the man his mother was planning to marry.

"He doesn't like me," Mike said. "He pretends he does, but he doesn't. That's why I'm down here."

Then Molly told them that she was sure her mother and father were going to get a divorce.

"Mrs. Mott?" asked Quincy. "And Mr. Mott?"

"That's right," Molly said. "I'm sure they are. That's why my father hasn't been down here at all this summer— haven't you noticed? He used to come down here every weekend and then spend all his vacation down here besides."

"I can't believe it," Quincy said.

"You better believe it," Molly said.

They all sat glumly in the sailboat, which was anchored up at the end of the bay.

"I guess my parents will be next," Quincy said. "They're

the only ones who aren't divorced already. But then maybe they won't. I think they've worked it out, or something. My mother just lets my father yell and goes on about her way. And he does all the cooking, and that pleases her. At least that's the way I've got it figured out.

"Maybe I'm not so bad off," Quincy said, "even if my family doesn't have the slightest interest in what I care about."

"Nobody's family cares about what anybody's interested in," Molly said. "I told you that. Families are a shuck."

"I guess we'd better get out and look some more, Mike," Quincy said. They jumped into the water, and Molly tossed the float to Mike and the inner tube to Quincy. (They were working with more expertise, Quincy thought.) Then Molly settled down in the stern of the boat under her big hat and raised an umbrella.

They saw no sign of a sunken Spanish ship that day either. In fact, they had seen very little on the bottom of the harbor at all . . . old tires . . . two sunken rowboats . . . millions of rusty cans and two big oil drums . . . and that was all.

"This is the biggest waste of time in the whole world," said Molly, as Mike and Quincy climbed back on board. Quincy and Mike shrugged, but then Molly said, "But what isn't?"

They headed for home.

"Low tide tonight! Low tide tonight!"

It was Grandpapa, acting like a town crier, waving his pipe instead of a bell.

He came over to the Luckies' house while Mr. Luckie was still cooking supper.

"Scalloping!" Jill cried.

Quincy joined in the jubilation. Scalloping was fun. You could only do it a few times a year at St. Jerome. You had to have a very low tide. During this low tide, the spits, which were grassy flats on the far side of Turtle Harbor near Turtle Point, were exposed. The water would be only a couple of inches deep on the spits, and you could walk around on them, and pick up scallops. The scallops weren't easy to see, but they betrayed their presence by sending up small jets of water from where they lay hidden under the grass.

Going scalloping was quite an undertaking. You had to have a boat to get out to the spits. You had to wear tennis shoes because the sharp grass and broken shells would cut your feet. Then you had to slosh around out on the spits, lifting up one heavy water-filled shoe and putting it down for each step, looking out for scallops, picking them up, and putting them in a bucket.

But it was worth the trouble. The scallops were the best in the world, or so everybody at St. Jerome believed.

Grandpapa organized the expedition to the spits, which would take place after supper. He would take his boat, he said, and he would make several trips since everybody wanted to go—Grandmama, the Standishes, and Mrs. Mott.

Sam said he'd sail over and somebody could go with him. Quincy chose to go with Grandpapa, and he said she could go on the first trip.

Quincy and her mother and Mrs. Mott and her grand-mother were in the first load.

Molly came down to see them off.

"Why aren't you coming, Molly?" Quincy asked her.

"I don't like to walk around out there in that old grass," Molly said.

"No sharks on the spits," Quincy said.

"You don't know what else is out there," Molly said.

"Silly!" Quincy said.

"Molly is so neurotic," Mrs. Mott sighed, as Grandpapa shoved the boat out. He got in and started the motor, which made too much noise for conversation. Quincy thought about Molly and Mrs. Mott. She thought Molly odd herself, but it made her mad for Mrs. Mott to call Molly "neurotic." Everybody was entitled to a little oddity, she thought.

When they got to the spits, Quincy jumped out and held the boat for the others. Then they all fanned out, walking with the exaggerated steps of Moon Walkers, lifting up first one heavy foot, then the next, stooping down to pick up a scallop, moving on.

Quincy picked up a few scallops and then saw the biggest whelk she'd ever seen. It was just lying there in the grass. She picked it up and put it in her bucket and thought of Mike Standish. She hoped somebody would remember to bring him out.

Then she saw an even larger Florida conch shell, and right beside it another. She picked them both up.

It was fantastic, and she showed them to Jill and Sam when they arrived in the sailboat.

They all agreed they'd seen big shells on the spits, but nothing like this before.

"It must still be the aftereffects of the storm," Mrs. Luckie said.

The scalloping was the best ever, too, they agreed.

When Grandpapa came back he brought the Standishes and Mike.

Mike was mildly interested in her big whelk and conchs and said he hoped he found some for his collection.

"You will," Quincy said. Mentally, she resolved to give Mike hers if he didn't find any.

They agreed it was very nasty work cleaning them—
you had to boil them and drag out the creature that in-
habited each one.

"Molly would never do it," Mike said.

They separated, each hunting alone. Quincy picked up
scallops as fast as she could. The spits were getting crowded.
People had come over from Turtle Point as well as St.
Jerome, and a dozen boats were anchored off the spits.
Dallas arrived in a boat from the marina and began to walk
along beside Melissa.

Quincy was watching them when she stumbled over the
bottle. She thought at first it was another large shell, but
when she picked it up she saw it was a bottle, an onion-
shaped bottle like ones in the pictures in the book on salvaging wrecks.

It was an old Spanish bottle. She slipped it into her bucket
among the scallops and didn't say anything about it.

When the water got deeper on the spits, Grandpapa
started taking people back to St. Jerome. Quincy would
have liked to have gone back with Dallas, who was taking
a boatload over to St. Jerome, but she hadn't been asked.
So she rode back with Mike and his grandparents.

Mike was more excited than Quincy had ever seen him.
He had found two sea horses on the spits—and a squid. He
showed them to her in the boat, and when they got on the
beach, away from the noise of the boat's motor, she con-
gratulated him.

"A squid!" Quincy said. "I never even saw one before."

"I wonder if your father would like to have it?" Mike
said. "They're good to eat."

"Squid?" Quincy said. "I don't know."

"On second thought, I think I'll try to keep it alive in my
aquarium. It's very unusual to find one so close to shore."

"You and your creatures!" said Quincy. (Mike didn't look as much like some of his creatures as he used to, she decided.) "You don't have any scallops!" she said.

"No," he said, "but I did find whelks and conchs—big ones," he said.

"Look at what I found," she said, and she showed him the bottle.

Mike knew at once that it was old and that it was Spanish. "Just like the ones in the book," he said. "There must be a wreck out there."

"I know," Quincy said.

She stuck the bottle back in with her scallops and started up the steps with it. When she got to her house, though, she took the bottle upstairs before she took her scallops around to the back porch where everybody was cleaning scallops.

Cleaning scallops was easy compared to cleaning crabs, Quincy thought. All you ate on the scallop was the little muscle that held the two shells together—but the muscle was on the outside and easy to cut off.

"We'll have a feast tomorrow," Mr. Luckie said.

Quincy hesitated to see if she was going to have to help with the scallops, decided she was safe, and started toward the front porch. She was in the kitchen when she heard her name called.

"Quincy!"

It was Dallas.

She went back on the porch.

"Where are you going?" he asked her.

"Just to get my telescope," she said. She hoped nobody would laugh at her.

"You have a telescope?" Dallas asked her.

"Oh, Ducky and that old telescope," Melissa said. "She's such a funny little ducky."

Dallas paid no attention to Melissa. "What kind of telescope do you have?" he asked Quincy.

"A two-inch refracting telescope," she said. "I think the magnification is about two hundred. I bought it at a garage sale. There wasn't anything wrong with it except one screw was loose. I tightened it."

"What are you going to look at tonight?" Dallas asked her.

"I'm looking at Messier objects," she said.

"That's good," Dallas said, nodding.

He was the very first person, Quincy thought, to whom she had ever mentioned anything in the sky who had the faintest interest or understanding of what she was talking about.

"What are Messier objects?" Jill asked.

"Nebulae," Quincy said. "A man listed them in a catalog. He was only interested in them because they weren't comets."

"Ducky has really enjoyed that telescope this summer," Mrs. Luckie said. "She found Jupiter and Mars—or what was it with the rings? Mercury?"

"That was Saturn, Mama," Quincy said, her teeth clenched. She turned and left the back porch.

Dallas followed her out to the front porch, where she took the telescope from its box.

"I always knew you were an interesting kid," Dallas said. "You're a real astronomy nut, aren't you?"

"As much as anybody can be in this family," Quincy said.

"What's wrong with your family?" Dallas said. "Oh, you mean because they're all into music and art and plays and that kind of thing?"

"Exactly," Quincy said.

"Well, you could be worse off," Dallas said. "My family doesn't even particularly care whether I go to college at all. They'd like to see me get a job on a shrimp boat."

"Everybody tells me horror tales about their parents," Quincy said. "I keep telling myself I'm not so bad off—but they sure do make me mad."

"Just don't let them get you down," Dallas said.

Quincy felt immeasurably cheered.

Sixteen

The next morning Quincy came downstairs and went on the porch to see if LeMoyne was out playing with the porpoises. He was.

Jill was on the front porch, picking her guitar.

"Look, Jill! LeMoyne is out there with the porpoises. I think that's the neatest thing about St. Jerome. . . ."

Jill smiled and went on picking.

Quincy went outside and stood on the edge of the bluff and watched LeMoyne. There were three porpoises out there, and LeMoyne would swim along beside one and then beside another. They seemed to be playing some kind of game, but Quincy couldn't figure out the rules.

After a while she went back in and asked Jill, "Do you think the porpoises really accept him, or does he just swim around out there with them?

"I don't know," Jill said. "Listen to this." She began to sing:

> "Oh, dock committee, serious group!
> Hail ye heroes, solemn troop!"

"What's that?" Quincy asked.

"It's a song for the Summer Show," Jill said.

"So you really are writing it yourselves this year," Quincy said.

"We're trying, but it's slow work. Why don't you help?"

"I can't," Quincy asid. "Did you write the music, too?"

"No, this one is to the tune of 'Hail, Columbia,' " Jill said. "But I'm having a hard time with the words."

"It's a great idea to write a song about that dumb dock committee," Quincy said. "I wish they'd get the dock rebuilt. I miss it."

"I know," Jill said. She hummed.

"Is the whole Show going to be about St. Jerome?" Quincy asked.

"The whole thing," Jill said. "Here's the theme song. Listen." She sang, to the tune of "Careless Love":

> "St. Jerome, oh, St. Jerome,
> St. Jerome, oh, St. Jerome,
> St. Jerome, oh, St. Jerome,
> We're back at St. Jerome once more."

Quincy thought that one was pretty monotonous, but she hated to tell Jill that.

"Come on, help me," Jill said. "You're full of bright ideas."

"Is it all songs?" Quincy asked.

"We want to have skits, little playlets, but we're having a hard time writing them. The songs are easiest."

"Why don't you have a song about LeMoyne?" Quincy asked.

"You do one," Jill said.

"I don't know how," Quincy said.

"Think about it," Jill said. "You like LeMoyne so much
—you're the one to write a song about him."

"What's Melissa doing for the Show?" Quincy asked.

"Lots," Jill said. "She's working on some scenery, for
one thing. And Dallas is going to rig up some lighting. We
never had any special lighting before."

"Terrific," said Quincy, but she felt as though she'd
wasted enough time. She went into the kitchen to get herself some breakfast.

Her father asked her to take some cleaned scallops down
to Miss Hattie Hawk's. "I don't think she was out on the
spits last night," he said.

Quincy took the plastic container of scallops and went
upstairs and got her bottle and went down to Miss Hattie
Hawk's house.

"Quincy, come in," said Miss Hattie Hawk. "I hear you
have a telescope. Did you know that telescopes are in the
finest tradition of St. Jerome? Old Mr. Belton Butler, who
used to own your house, had a telescope. He kept it on the
porch upstairs."

"How could he look at the stars from the porch?"
Quincy asked.

"Oh, he didn't use it for stars," Miss Hattie Hawk said.
"He liked to look at boats in Turtle Harbor and out in the
Gulf."

Quincy thought it would be pretty dull to look at boats,
but she didn't say so. "Look what I found," she said. She
showed her the bottle.

"It's an onion bottle," Miss Hattie Hawk said. It was a
typical Spanish wine bottle and very old, she added. "And
you found it on the spits?" she said. "Well, everything
washes up out there. There must be a Spanish ship out there.

If I ever get back to town, I'll try to do some research to see if there's a record anywhere of a Spanish ship that went down near here."

As always, Quincy was cheered by Miss Hattie Hawk. Then she remembered to ask her what she thought of her grandfather's shark line.

"Does no harm," said Miss Hattie Hawk. "If your grandfather enjoys it, let him fiddle with it."

When she met Molly and Mike on the beach, Molly said she didn't want to go out searching anymore. "There's no wreck out there, and if there is, we'll never find it," she said.

Quincy told her about the bottle, but that didn't change Molly's mind.

"We've covered Turtle Harbor inch by inch," Molly said, "and if there's a sunken ship out there, you can't see it from the surface."

"It seems such a sure thing to me," Quincy said. "The coins. The bottle. The piece of blue-and-white china."

"If we found the wreck, we'd still have problems," Mike said. "We'd need divers and scuba equipment and stuff like that."

"But we would have *found* it," Quincy said.

"Everybody says we're silly to look for a wreck," Molly said.

"Who's everybody?" Quincy asked.

"My mom," Molly said.

"Did you tell your mother about this?" Quincy asked her angrily.

"I had to," Molly said. "She kept asking what the three of us were doing out there all day long. She finally wormed it out of me."

Quincy was furious and unhappy that Molly had talked about the search. It wasn't just that Miss Hattie Hawk had said to keep it a secret, but that grown people would laugh. In the beginning, it had all seemed so reasonable, but they hadn't accomplished one single thing, Quincy thought. It was terrible to have a good idea—and have it come to nothing.

Suddenly, Quincy had a new idea.

"Look," she said, "the ship may not be in Turtle Harbor at all. It's out in the Gulf! It wouldn't have come in here! It must be out in the Gulf—that's why the bottle washed up on the spits. Let's go out in the Gulf and look!"

"You mean sail out in your boat?" Molly asked.

"Why not?" Quincy said. "We could try. The wreck is probably just on the other side of Turtle Point—maybe down a little—and the current would wash stuff into the beaches here. You know how crazy currents are."

"I don't want to go sailing in the Gulf," Molly said. "Not in this dinky little boat."

"You don't really like to go sailing anywhere," Quincy said. "And if it were a royal yacht, you wouldn't like it any better."

"Probably not," Molly agreed.

"You are so lazy, Molly Mott!" Quincy said.

"That's what everybody says," Molly said. "And I say it myself. I don't like to *do* things. Why is everybody always trying to get me to do things?"

"I don't know, Molly. I give up," said Quincy.

They were all quiet for a moment, and then Quincy said, "Well, thanks for helping, anyway. I'm sorry it didn't turn out better. I appreciate your help."

"That's okay," Mike said. "I kind of believe in it."

"Well, it wasn't all bad," Molly said cheerfully. "My mother was very pleased with all my activity for a while."

They started across the beach.

"Look at Petey!" Quincy said.

"He loves to chase sand crabs," Mike said. "He never gets tired of it, as old as he is. And he tries to dig them out."

Petey was digging frantically in the sand. He had dug up something gold. Quincy could see it glitter.

"It's another coin!" she said, picking it up. She handed it to Molly. "Here, you can have this one, keep it. I have several others."

"Really?" Molly said. "Is it a real Spanish gold piece?"

"Like the others," Quincy said. "Don't you see, Molly? There's got to be a wreck around. These gold pieces are coming from somewhere."

"Oh, all right," Molly said. "I'll go out in the Gulf. I love this gold piece."

"It's silly not to try," Mike said. "Let's go."

Seventeen

They set out that morning with an unusual excitement and a little spice of fear. Quincy wished she were a better sailor. She had never taken the boat out into the open Gulf—and Molly and Mike were not even as experienced as she was. Oh, well, it was a nice calm day, she thought.

They tacked up to the end of Turtle Harbor, then headed down toward the tip of Turtle Point. As they glided past the marina, Quincy looked hard to see if she could catch a glimpse of Dallas Truitt. No sign of him. No sign of life at all, as a matter of fact, at the marina.

They started around the tip of Turtle Point. "Oh, there's that rip current right at the end of the Point," she said. "I don't want to get caught in that. . . ."

Just as she spoke, they were caught in it. She'd come too close to the land. . . . She let the boat swing around into the wind, and the current carried it swiftly back into Turtle Harbor. Quincy simply waited until it was out of the current and in the comparatively still water of the bay and then started over, heading farther west, to avoid the current, then coming about and heading for the Gulf.

She felt very proud of herself—she had kept calm and had managed the boat properly.

"That's a terrible little current," she said. "We came over here a long time ago and had a picnic right there on the beach at the very tip of Turtle Point. We would jump in the water there at one end of the little channel on the Gulf side, and the current would carry us, with us standing straight up, right around the tip of the Point to the harbor side. It was super fun. Then somebody told my parents that was very dangerous, that current. But I think it all depends on the tide and the weather, or something."

By now they were well out from land in the Gulf. The expanse of water looked very large. It looked vast. And Quincy, a child raised on a steady diet of Shakespeare, thought of the line "Spirits from the vasty deep" from *Henry IV*. She shivered.

"How do we look out here?" Mike asked. "This is a mighty large area to cover. How do we start?"

"It's hopeless," Molly said.

"We can just go up and down the coast," Quincy said. "We can do that easily with the wind blowing offshore like it is . . . and we can look the same way we did inside the harbor."

Quincy jumped over the side of the boat, and Molly handed her the inner tube. She climbed up on it and, lying across the tube, began to paddle, looking down at the bottom. The water was clearer out here than it had been in the harbor, and the bottom seemed cleaner. Quincy had had so much experience she could paddle and look for almost endless periods of time. Her back and shoulders were not tan, but a deep mahogany brown after the hours of searching. Poor Mike had at first burned badly and then peeled. But he had persevered, and worn a T-shirt while he was in the sun. Now he was beginning to be very brown, too.

Molly moved the boat for them several times, and Mike and Quincy ranged around in a wide area. The novelty of being outside the harbor and in the Gulf was exciting to them, and they kept at it steadily.

After a long time, though, Quincy noticed that the waves were getting rougher and that a big black cloud was building up over the land.

She called to Mike, and they paddled back to the boat and clambered in.

Quincy took the tiller and picked up the mainsheet, ready to shift the boat to catch the offshore wind and run back into the harbor.

But the wind had shifted. It was coming from land. And the clouds over the shore were getting bigger and blacker.

"Oh, good grief!" Quincy said.

"What's the matter?" Molly asked. She was instantly alert to the faint note of anxiety in Quincy's voice.

"Well, the wind has shifted," she said. "We might have a hard time getting in." She looked at the sky again. "And it looks like it's going to storm."

"Quincy, I'm scared," Molly said.

Quincy said nothing. She was scared, too. She was scared to death, to tell the truth. The wind felt cold and mean on her wet shoulders. She had no confidence in her ability to handle the boat in a storm, and Molly and Mike were dependent on her. Oh, Lord, she thought, why did I ever do such a dumb thing as this? And why didn't I keep watching the sky?

She began to try to head to shore and wondered how

close she could get to the wind, which was blowing in exactly the opposite direction she wanted to go. What was safe in a situation like this, and what wasn't?

"Are we in any danger, Quincy?" Mike asked her, and his voice broke when he said the word "danger."

They are so scared it makes me scared, Quincy thought. I'm scared anyway—what am I thinking about? Oh, Lord, what was that hymn they sang so often at the Baptist church in Elysium? It had one line, "For those in peril on the sea . . ." and it seemed appropriate.

The waves were rougher now, and the tops of them were white with foam. The cloud was closer, and the wind was stronger and blowing in gusts.

Quincy tacked as far west as she thought was necessary and said, "Ready, coming about," and they all ducked, and Quincy prayed, and the boat swung about and headed east, with Quincy steering it as close to the north—and the shore —as she could. It was very hard to hold the boat steady on course, and Quincy was tempted to just give up, let the boat turn into the wind, the sail flop loose, and ride out the storm that was about to strike them. No, she thought. Better not. Better keep on trying. She hung on to the tiller and held the sheet as tightly as she dared.

And then it happened. A really strong blast of wind hit them.

The boat jibed.

The boom snapped across, hitting Mike in the head and missing Molly, who was cowering in the bottom of the boat. And as the boom swung, the momentum and the wind conspired to flip the boat over on its side, and all three of them went into the water.

Quincy surfaced and looked around. The boat was lying

sullenly on its side. It was raining. It was thundering. Lightning was flashing. The wind was blowing, and it was cold. The warm and friendly Gulf had become the enemy.

Where were the others? Were they caught under the sail? Quincy wondered. She was worried about Mike—she was sure the boom had hit him in the head. There he was, looking dazed. But his eyes were open and his head was at least above water. Thank heavens I made everybody wear life jackets, Quincy thought.

Molly was swimming doggedly toward the boat. Of course, Molly had known how to swim well for years. She just hadn't bothered to swim any this year—but at least she hadn't atrophied.

"We can hang on the boat," Quincy shouted. "It won't sink." The other two joined her.

"It's hard to hang on," Molly said.

Molly looked ghastly, Quincy thought. Green.

"Use the handle on the stern," Quincy suggested. "Are you all right?" she asked Mike. "I thought the boom hit you."

"It did, but I'm all right, I guess," Mike said. He rubbed his head. "I'm getting a lump. Feel it."

Quincy reached over and felt it. The lump was already as big as an egg.

"Dammit, I can hardly swim at all," Mike said. "I'm scared."

"I don't think," Quincy said, and she spoke very slowly and carefully, "I don't think there's any need to be frightened." She paused. "I think we'll—be—all—right." She wasn't terribly sure herself, and so she said the words very slowly so she could stop if she decided she was being overly optimistic. She felt responsible for them all being out in the

Gulf, she felt responsible for capsizing the boat, and she didn't want to hold out false hopes at this point. "If—we—can—just—hang—on—until—the storm—is—over," she went on, "somebody will see us and take us in."

"How long will it last?" Mike said.

"I don't think it will last long," Quincy said. "You know these summer thundershowers haven't been lasting long."

She listened to herself talking and thought she sounded like a parent reassuring a nervous child. Oh, God, I wish I had a parent to soothe me, she thought fleetingly. It was terrible to be the leader. I don't want to grow up, she thought. I really don't. It's going to be awful to be grown.

A lightning bolt seemed to crack right over them, and the sound of thunder was immediate and immensely loud. They all screamed.

"I thought we were hit," Molly said.

It was odd she was the first to speak, Quincy thought. Maybe Molly would be all right. "I did, too," she said out loud.

"But we weren't," Mike said.

They all felt oddly cheered that they'd survived such an unbelievably fierce flash of lightning and percussion of thunder.

"There's your sun hat over there," Quincy said to Molly. "I guess the float and all our stuff got away."

"I don't need the hat now," Molly said.

"I'm going to swim over and get it for you," Quincy said.

"Why?"

"Because this storm is going to be over in a minute and you'll get sunburned bad if you don't have it," Quincy said.

"Wait a minute, Quincy," Molly said. "Wait until it quits thundering, anyway."

"Okay," Quincy said, but she kept an eye on the hat as it bobbed nearby. She would watch it disappear behind a a wave and then see it reappear. It gave her something to do besides worry about what was going to happen to them.

"I hope this isn't another hurricane," said Mike.

Quincy's stomach dropped suddenly at the thought. "Oh, it's not," she said. "It came from over land. I saw it."

"You're right," Mike said.

"Besides, it couldn't strike this suddenly," Molly said. "Alberta was on the radio days before it hit."

"Does anyone know we're out in the Gulf?" Quincy asked. "We didn't tell anybody, did we?"

"We didn't know ourselves," Mike said.

"That's right," Quincy said.

"They knew you took the boat," Molly said. "And when they look and don't see us in Turtle Harbor. . . ."

"They may think we've put into shore someplace," Quincy said.

"Oh, they know we never put into shore," Molly said. "My mother knows I'm afraid of snakes."

"Yeah, but she's seen you start going out in a boat all of a sudden," Quincy said.

"I believe they'll come look for us," Molly said. "You know how parents are."

"I know I hope they're like that," Quincy said.

"And grandparents, too," Mike said.

The storm was passing over, Quincy decided. The water was calmer and the thunder was much, much farther away. "I'm going after your hat," she said.

She started swimming and found it terribly hard going

in the heavy waves. But she really wanted to get Molly her hat. It had become a symbol, the necessity to get that hat for Molly.

She swam and swam. Each wave was like a mountain, and just as she would reach out to get the hat, another mountain would pour down and wash it out of her reach. She kept on, though, until she had it in her hand, and she swam slowly back to the boat.

"Oh, thank you, Quincy," Molly said. "Now I hope the sun comes out in a hurry."

"So do I," Mike said, "so somebody will come pull us in."

Molly tied her hat to the handle on the stern of the boat. "Do you know," she said, "I just this minute thought about sharks?" She gave another scream—not as loud as the one she'd screamed when the lightning almost hit them, but a substantial scream, nevertheless. She looked green again.

"Look, Molly, you didn't think about sharks for a whole long time, so don't think about them now," Quincy said. "Please." Quincy looked at her beseechingly. "Please don't start thinking about sharks."

"I can't help it," Molly said. Tears were running down her cheeks again. "I can't help but think about the awful things that are down here under my feet." She began to sob.

Her genuine terror was unnerving Quincy. She began to remember the awful shark in *Jaws*.

"Knock it off!" It was Mike who spoke to Molly. "Don't act like that. You'll scare Quincy, too. It is extremely unlikely that a shark will attack us, so just forget it. And if a shark does attack us, we might as well die bravely."

"We're not going to *die*," Quincy said with disgust. "We're going to hang on here until we get picked up. That's all."

Molly stopped sobbing, but she looked miserable.

"Feel the knot on Mike's head," Quincy said. "He's being very brave."

Molly felt the knot and shuddered. But she wasn't crying anymore.

"Listen," Quincy said, "you know what? I think I'll swim into shore and get help!"

"Swim into shore!" Molly was startled. She didn't even look green now.

"Yes," Quincy said. "You know, like Mr. Charlie Standish—Mike's father—did that time. You've heard that story."

"But you wouldn't take a shower before you told anybody, would you?" Molly asked. She even giggled.

"Of course I wouldn't," Quincy said. "Look, I wouldn't have to do all he did. He swam into Turtle Point, walked across the Point, and then swam across the harbor to St. Jerome. I guess that's before they built all the houses on Turtle Point. I'll just swim to the Point and go to the marina. You can see it from here. I'll swim right toward it, and I'll get help right away."

"Are you sure that's a good idea?" Mike asked. "Won't somebody be along pretty soon?"

"Well, if somebody comes along, you can get them to pick me up, too," Quincy said. "But you know it might be a long time until somebody sees out here and gets us. I'm a very good swimmer, and I have on a life jacket. If I get tired, I'll just float. I'll swim straight toward the marina, so you'll know where I am. I'd rather be doing something— and that way we know we'll get help eventually."

"I feel like I should do it," Mike said, "since I'm the only male."

"But you're a rotten swimmer," Quincy said.

119

"I know it," Mike said.

"And I don't mind," Quincy said. "I really don't."

She let go of the boat and reached out and hugged Molly, who hugged her back (and quickly grabbed the boat again). She shook hands with Mike and said, "Well, I'm off."

"Bon voyage," Mike said.

The water was already calmer than it had been when she went after the hat, and swimming toward the shore seemed easier than swimming about in the open water trying to grab a hat.

She swam slowly so as not to waste her energy, and she tried not to fool around. When she got tired, she swam on her back for a while and noticed that the sky was clearing. She swam on her left side and then on her right side and then turned back over on her stomach and did the breast stroke for a while. She even attempted the butterfly, but gave it up after a few strokes—it was too exhausting. She did the plain old front crawl for a while and then rested again and merely dog-paddled for a long time . . . but she could tell she was slowly, very slowly, getting closer to land.

She could now tell that the main, big metal building of the marina was blue. For a long time, it had been just a gray blur.

She swam on and began to feel heroic. She pushed out all thought of sharks—Molly was really very alarming on that subject. She swam on. She thought again of Mr. Charlie Standish swimming into shore. It had been more than twenty years ago, she thought, and now his son was clinging to the boat while somebody else—and a girl, at that—was swimming into shore for help.

120

She thought of lots of things. She thought about the stars and the planets and about all the nebulae she wanted to see . . . she thought about the paired stars . . . she thought about her family and how uninterested they were in science . . . how Melissa patronized her and how her father thought it was a phase that would pass . . . how her mother tried, but couldn't even remember that it was Saturn that had rings . . . about Sam, whom she hardly ever saw this summer . . . and about Jill, who was really her favorite in the family, and her songs . . . and about the Summer Show.

She looked at the coast. The marina looked no closer this time. This was a very long swim. How far out was the boat? She rolled over and looked back and couldn't see it. How long was all this taking? What time was it? What if it got dark? But it couldn't get dark, could it? They had gone out in the morning, and surely it wouldn't get dark while she was swimming to shore. It would be awful to be out in the Gulf in the dark.

She resolutely put down her fears, and swam. Of course, it wouldn't get dark. It probably wasn't even the middle of the afternoon yet. She turned over on her back and decided the sun was about to come out from behind a cloud. The cloud was sailing past the sun, and as soon as it sailed a little farther the sun would shine.

The sun broke out while she watched, but then another scallop of cloud covered it up. Quincy was disappointed. She turned back on her stomach and did the crawl.

She looked at the water about her and thought of the Ancient Mariner . . . "Water, water everywhere and not a drop to drink."

She was really thirsty. How good it would be to get home

121

and have something cool to drink. Or something warm to drink. She thought about all the things she liked to drink—water, milk, orange juice, lemonade, apple juice, grape juice, cranberry juice, Hawaiian Punch, Kool-Aid, Coca-Cola, ginger ale, chocolate milk, ice tea, hot chocolate . . . the list was endless. Water would be best, she decided, nice, clear, not salty water.

Water was hydrogen and oxygen, and hydrogen and oxygen were gasses, and yet they made this liquid . . . and there were all these molecules of oxygen and hydrogen in this water.

And seawater had the same ratio of salt to water that human blood did. Man came from the sea, she thought. She had always thought this was a rather romantic concept, that man had some seawater in his veins, and it had almost reconciled her to the beach at times . . . but she was tired of seawater. If she had stayed in Houston, she thought, this would never have happened.

Florida was downright dangerous, she thought. You could get killed fooling around with boats and things. Especially sailboats. A motorboat would never have turned over. You had to do something really silly to make a motorboat turn over, but a sailboat was a chancy thing.

She rested on her back again, and the cloud slid past and the sun came out and she felt much better. She swam on and on. She was tired and she was thirsty. She was thirsty and tired of being in water over her head. Her fingers and her toes were wrinkled, and she felt as though she would never be dry again.

Maybe she should have stayed with the boat. Wasn't that a safety maxim? Yet it had seemed important to *do* something. The captain always goes down with the boat, and she was the captain. Well, she hadn't gone down or stayed with the boat.

She would probably get in trouble for taking the boat out in the Gulf without permission. This was the first summer she'd ever really used the sailboat, and nobody had bothered to shout the rules at her.

She swam and she swam. Her arms ached. She felt as though she were standing off somewhere and watching herself swim and hearing herself think, I am very tired. I am very tired.

She rolled over on her back to float and rest. I can float just like Mama, she thought. Like mother, like daughter.

The waves washed her about gently as she floated. Maybe if she waited here, somebody would come by and pick her up. No, that was ridiculous. Nobody would ever see one lone person floating out here—that was for sure.

She made herself turn over on her stomach and swim again. Then she rested on her stomach and just kicked. That should propel her forward. When she looked up, though, she realized she had been going astray, heading westward down the beach toward St. Lucy. She pulled toward the right, toward the marina, and swam hard. The marina was looking larger and bluer and clearer. She could make out the individual houses strung out along Turtle Point now. She was getting closer. She looked back out to sea and could see no sign of the overturned boat.

Eventually, she got close enough to shore that she could feel the inward rush of waves toward the beach, and that helped a lot. She could float from time to time and know she was still being propelled toward land.

Then she had a moment of panic. The current was toward the shore, but also toward the west, and what if the current pulled her past the marina and the tip of Turtle Point? She'd never be able to swim back up against the current. And she didn't think she could swim all the way to St. Jerome.

It would be really awful if she missed Turtle Point. She'd just have to relax and let the current carry her all the way to St. Lucy. She would just walk up the lawn of one of those houses at St. Lucy and somebody would take her to get help. Call the Coast Guard.

She had to laugh at the thought of the Coast Guard. The nearest Coast Guard station was in Panama City, and the Coast Guard auxiliary at Elysium was a bunch of fishermen —and they'd all be out fishing.

Captain Bite was the head of the Coast Guard auxiliary. He was the brother of the Mr. Bite who was going to re-build the St. Jerome dock. He wore an ancient, dirty old yachting cap and liked to tell tall tales. But he was respected as a good fisherman and a knowledgeable seaman. She would love to see Captain Bite and his boat pull up beside her.

She swam hard to the right to offset the pull of the cur-rent and noticed that waves were breaking all around her. She was on the sandbar!

She put her feet down and stood up.

She was standing on the earth—not dry land, but the earth was beneath her feet and God was in his heaven.

She had swum out to the sandbar before . . . sometimes they used to come to the beach on Turtle Point to play in the surf, and she'd been out this far lots of times. It was quite an adventure, though, to swim out as far as the sand-bar. And now she had swum *in* to the sandbar. And all that remained to be done was something she'd done before, something she knew she could do.

She could easily recognize the houses directly in front of her, and the marina was only slightly to the left.

She walked toward the shore as far as she could until the sandbar ended and the water got deep again. Then she swam until she reached shallow water again and stood up, trembling. She walked through the breaking waves to the damp sand of the beach.

She sat down on the sand and rested just a minute, and let the sun dry her hair. There was no sign of a storm now. And the sun was still high in the sky.

She walked across the beach and through the dunes and suddenly stepped on a sandspur. She'd forgotten about sandspurs. They didn't have them at St. Jerome. She pulled the spur out of her foot and walked on, now watching out for them.

She got to the hot asphalt of the road and realized it was only fifty feet down the road to the marina. She ran across the pavement and hit the sand on the other side of it and walked down the road.

Her heart was beating very fast. Her hair was drying out and felt very sticky and heavy with salt water. She had that baked feeling you always got when you didn't take a shower and rinse off the salt water. And so much salt water! She knew, at last, how Charlie Standish had felt. She wanted a shower more than anything else, but she stepped resolutely into the cool shade of the big marina building.

After her eyes adjusted to the dim light, she saw Dallas Truitt over in a corner working on a boat with another man.

"Dallas!" she called.

He looked up, puzzled. He frowned. She thought he didn't recognize her.

"It's Quincy," she said. "Quincy Luckie."

"Hi," he said. He put down his tools and started toward her. "I couldn't recognize you with the light behind you like that," he said. "What are you doing over here?" He looked her over from head to toe, the sticky hair, the wet bathing suit, the bare feet.

"Our boat turned over," she said. "Out in the Gulf."

"Where? Are you all right? Who-all was with you?"

"Right out there," she said. "I'm okay. I swam in. But Mike Standish and Molly Mott are still out there. Hanging on the boat."

"Come on," Dallas said. "Let's go get them." He wiped his hands on his dungarees and said to the man with whom he'd been working, "Boat turned over out there, Buddy. We better go take the big boat and pull them in." He turned to Quincy. "Do you have enough rope out there to tow the boat in? Oh, no telling what happened to everything. I'll get some rope." He went into a storeroom and got a coil of rope.

"Do we need anybody else?" Buddy asked. "We could call Elysium and get somebody to come help."

"I think we can do it," Dallas said.

They all walked outside to the dock and got inside the big marina boat, and Dallas started the engine with no trouble. The big boat whirred out of the marina dock area and into Turtle Harbor, and they rode swiftly around the tip of Turtle Point and out into the Gulf.

"Now, where is it?" Dallas asked her.

Quincy pointed.

"And you swam all the way in?" Dallas asked her.

"Yes," Quincy said. "Was I wrong? Should I have stayed with the boat?"

126

"Yes," Dallas said. "But you're very brave, Quincy. You're a brave girl. Most girls would be hollering and crying and carrying on."

Quincy immediately began to cry.

"I'm sorry. I shouldn't have mentioned it," Dallas said.

"It's just that I'm so thirsty," Quincy said, wiping her eyes. "I thought I would never make it to the shore and I was so thirsty."

Buddy reached into a plastic cooler in the bottom of the boat and brought out a Dr. Pepper and handed it to her. Quincy ordinarily hated Dr. Pepper, but she grabbed the can from Buddy and desperately tried to open it. She broke the ring off and thought she'd cry again from frustration, but Buddy had already fished out another can of Dr. Pepper. He opened it for her and handed it to her. She gulped it.

"It's the best thing I ever drank in my life," she said.

"I see 'em," Dallas said, and he headed the boat toward the capsized sailboat. Molly was wearing her sun hat now, and she and Mike were still clinging to the boat.

They both waved wildly at the marina boat.

Quincy and Buddy and Dallas waved back.

"Lord a-mercy," Dallas said. "The mast didn't break. You just flipped it over, did you?"

"I jibed," Quincy said dolefully. "When the storm came up, all of a sudden, I just jibed. I'm sorry."

"Happens to the best of sailors," Buddy said. "Don't you feel bad about it."

They had a problem. Molly wouldn't let go of the sailboat to swim to the marina boat. Finally, Dallas told her he'd go off and leave her if she didn't let go and swim to where they could pull her in. She paddled over and they hauled her over the side like a big fish.

127

They threw a rope to Mike, who tied it to the stern. "I think we better tow her a little ways—to the sandbar, anyway—so we can turn her right-side-up," Buddy said.

They pulled Mike in and headed slowly back toward Turtle Point, towing the boat awkwardly on its side. It was hard to pull—it swung heavily at the end of the rope—but at last they got to shallow water near the sandbar. Dallas and Buddy and Mike and Quincy all got out and heaved and pushed until they got the sailboat upright. The mast came up with the wet sail flapping mightily, but it was all right.

"Good little boat," Dallas said. "She's all there."

Buddy thought Quincy ought to get back in the sailboat and hold the tiller while they towed it to the marina dock. "Unless you want to sail it on home," he said.

"NO!" said Quincy. "No."

She climbed in the sailboat—nobody would ever know how much she hated to get back into it—and Dallas threw her a can to bail with. The sailboat was full of water and sat heavily in the waves.

She began to bail, but it was going to take a long time to bail out that boat.

She held the tiller while the motorboat pulled her slowly around the sandbar, around the tip of Turtle Point, and into Turtle Harbor and, finally, into the marina dock area.

"I'll borrow a car and take you home," Dallas said. "Can I use your car, Buddy?"

"Sure," Buddy said, and they all walked through the marina building and got into Buddy's car, which was a marvelous cerise-colored Pontiac with enormous tires and a cut-out muffler that roared fiercely as they sped the length of Turtle Point and through Elysium around to St. Jerome.

"Well, here you are," Dallas said, as he pulled up behind the Luckie house.

"Thank you so much, Dallas," Quincy said. "You're pure gold."

Molly and Mike thanked him, and he assured them it was his pleasure. "No trouble at all, and we were glad to do it," he said.

"Well, I guess I'll go in and face the music," Quincy said.

"You want us to come in with you?" Molly said.

Quincy smiled at Molly and—suddenly—hugged her. Molly was brave in her own way. "Molly, I'm sorry I did it to you. And I'm glad you didn't get bit by a shark."

"Thanks," Molly said.

"Maybe it cured you," Quincy said. "Maybe you'll be going in swimming every day again."

"I won't either," Molly said. "But don't feel badly. Really." She turned and started toward her own house.

"I'm sorry, Mike," she said.

"It's okay," Mike said. "I just hope your folks won't get mad at you."

"I'll survive," Quincy said.

Eighteen

When Quincy went in the house it was very quiet. The kitchen was a mess, with dirty dishes all over the table, the stove, and the sink.

She walked through the empty living room and out onto the big screened front porch. Not a soul around. Where was everybody? Oh, well, she thought, now she could take a shower. She went to the outside shower and stood under the warm, clear water for a long time, washing her hair twice.

Wrapped in a towel, she came back inside and went upstairs and put on shorts and a clean shirt. Then she brushed her hair and put some of Melissa's moisturizer on her face. She went downstairs and, ignoring the mess in the kitchen, fixed herself a peanut butter sandwich and drank a glass of milk. Then she took a banana from the fruit bowl on the table and walked out to the front lawn. Everybody seemed to be on the beach. Her mother was standing there, fists clenched at her side, gazing out to sea. Sam and Jill were sitting on the sand. Her grandmother and Mrs. Standish were walking up and down.

Quincy realized they were looking for the boat. They're worried about us, she said to herself.

She went down the steps to the beach, hurrying, and called, "Here I am!"

Everybody turned and stared, and then began to babble. "Where's Michael?" Mrs. Standish said. "Where's Michael?"

"At your house, I guess," Quincy said. "Dallas brought us back in a car from the marina and let us out in the back. Mike's okay. Molly's okay. I'm okay—I just took a shower."

"But what HAPPENED?" Mrs. Luckie asked.

"We capsized," Quincy said. "Out in the Gulf. But nobody got hurt. The boat's all right. I swam in to Turtle Point and got Dallas and he went out and towed the boat in. It's okay. It's at the marina. And he brought us home in Buddy's car."

"Why didn't you come right down here and tell us you were all right?" Mrs. Luckie shouted. Quincy had never heard her mother shout like that. It was frightening. "How could you be so inconsiderate? What do you mean fooling around up there taking a shower?" And Mrs. Luckie burst into tears and threw her arms around Quincy.

Grandmama hugged them both. Mrs. Standish ran off— to see about Mike, Quincy supposed.

"Oh, Ducky! Quincy! I'm sorry. But I was sooo worried," gasped Mrs. Luckie. "I'm sorry I shouted at you. Have you had anything to eat?" But she wouldn't let go of Quincy and Quincy hated to push her mother's arms away—but she couldn't breathe, much less answer her.

"Oh, Quincy!" her mother kept on saying, still hugging her.

"Mama, let go of her," Jill said. "She's all right. Grandpapa's gone in his boat to look for you-all with Mr. Standish, and Papa's gone to call the Coast Guard. Quincy, did you really swim to Turtle Point? How far out were you?"

"I don't know," Quincy said. "It was a long swim."

Mrs. Luckie at last let go of Quincy and stood back and looked at her. "Well, let's go back up to the house . . . you're sure you're all right, Quincy? And the other children are all right, too?"

"Mike got hit in the head with the boom, but he's all right," Quincy said. "Molly's fine. She stayed in the water for hours—or it seemed like hours. As scared as she was, I thought she was pretty brave, as scared as she was."

Everybody laughed at this, but then everybody explained they knew exactly what Quincy meant.

They sat down on the front porch, and Mrs. Luckie brought ice tea for everybody. Grandmama brought over some gingerbread she'd baked. "I know your father doesn't like it, Quincy," she said, "but I know you do, so you eat it all up."

Quincy ate gingerbread and drank tea and told them all about the capsizing in great detail.

Everyone agreed that Quincy had been very brave.

"But you should not have taken the sailboat out into the Gulf without telling us," said Mrs. Luckie. She was beginning to get mad all over again. "You haven't had enough sailing experience. . . ."

"Oh, Mama, don't fuss at her," Jill said. "She's learned her lesson."

"And taking a shower—while I was down there on the beach going crazy!" said Mrs. Luckie.

"Mama, that was just like Mr. Charlie Standish," Quincy said. "What I really wanted to do was take a shower before I told them at the marina about the boat."

"Oh, Lord, I wish I'd never told that story . . . to think you swam in like Charlie Standish!"

About that time Papa arrived, looking white around the mouth and not shouting at all. "They said they'd go out to look for them," he said. "They said they'd bring them home as soon as they found them. . . ."

He saw Quincy and stopped with his mouth hanging open. Then his face lit up and he smiled. Then he shouted, "Where have you been? What did you do with the boat?"

Quincy told her story again.

"Good God! You've got no business to take that boat out into the Gulf with those two little nincompoops. You're not a nincompoop, but you sure can act like one. What do you think you were doing out there anyway? You weren't fishing."

"Just messing around," Quincy said.

"Why couldn't you mess around inside the bay where we could see you?" asked Mr. Luckie. "Answer me! Answer me!"

Quincy was getting used to people's reactions. First they were relieved and then they got mad. She was getting tired of their shouting.

"We were looking for treasure!" she said.

"Treasure! Good God Almighty!" her father said.

"What kind of treasure?" her mother asked.

"A sunken Spanish ship," Quincy said. "You remember those coins I found after the storm? Well, I found some more. And I found a bottle on the spits that's an old Spanish bottle. We think there's a ship out there somewhere, and we couldn't find it inside Turtle Harbor, so we went out in the Gulf."

"You couldn't get a treasure up from the bottom of the

sea," Mr. Luckie said. "You don't have diving equipment. Are you insane?"

"We knew we couldn't bring it up," said Quincy, "but I read about a man who found a wrecked Spanish ship by paddling around on a float with a homemade snorkeling mask . . . it was off the east coast of Florida."

Then Mr. Luckie, as though he couldn't believe in the idea of a treasure ship, changed the subject. "You shouldn't have left the boat when it capsized," he said.

"I know," Quincy said. "But Mr. Charlie Standish did—and it was cold and I felt bad about Molly being out there, as scared as she is, and I just wanted to get help in a hurry."

"And you shouldn't have gone out in the Gulf without knowing how to sail better," Mr. Luckie said. "We always check everybody out before they can take a boat out in the Gulf."

"Nobody ever said anything to me about being checked out," Quincy said. "Nobody paid much attention to me this summer—except to devil me about the Summer Show. I didn't even want to come. I just tried to make the best of it—and I kind of enjoyed looking for treasure." Quincy was tired and she had used all the willpower and self-control she could muster. She couldn't keep from crying. She began to sob. "You never pay me any attention."

"We do," her father said.

"Maybe she's right," Mrs. Luckie said. "I didn't bother to check her out in the boat. I didn't pay any attention to what they were doing."

"You always take her side!" Mr. Luckie said.

Now her parents were arguing. Quincy hated it when they started arguing. She'd rather they'd shout at her than shout at each other. She began to cry harder.

"I'm sorry, Ducky," her father said. He came over and

took her in his arms and held her close. "I'm really sorry. You're great. You're a brave girl to swim in to shore . . . even if you should have stayed with the boat. . . . No, I mean, you're brave, period."

"I'm sorry," Quincy said. "I really am."

"That's okay," Mr. Luckie said, "but if you're going to use the boat, you'll have to obey the rules. You must always check out with me or your mother, tell us where you're going. Always be sure that everybody wears a ski belt or a life jacket—"

"I did that!" Quincy said. "I always did that!"

"Thank God for that," Mr. Luckie said. "Also you should check the weather on the radio before you go, and watch the sky constantly . . . good sailors always watch the sky. But anyway, I think you ought to stay inside Turtle Harbor for a while, until you're more experienced at handling the boat. Something serious could happen in the Gulf."

"Yeah," Sam said, "you could break the mast off next time. That would be very expensive."

"I was thinking of Ducky herself," Mr. Luckie said reprovingly. "And Molly and Mike. Their lives are more important than the mast. Although, I must say it would be very bad if you stove up the boat, Ducky." He smiled at Quincy as he said this.

"Yes, sir," Quincy said.

Mr. Luckie kept on talking to her about the boat. Quincy sat and listened and nodded. She rather enjoyed being the center of attention as long as nobody was shouting. Her mother kept reaching over and holding her hand, and her father kept looking at her the whole time he was talking to her. Jill and Sam sat there, too, and didn't wander off.

Mr. Luckie had to leave to go pick up Melissa at work,

135

and he asked Quincy what she wanted for supper. Quincy chose steak.

"Steak!" Mr. Luckie said. "Not seafood?"

"I am very tired of seafood," Quincy said. "I'd love steak."

"All right," Mr. Luckie said. "The beef they sell at Mr. Willow's store in Elysium leaves a great deal to be desired, but I will do the best I can."

He left.

Quincy told her story for her grandfather, and then again when Melissa got home.

"Well, we'll have to go get the sailboat, if it's still over at the marina," Melissa said.

They were all discussing the logistics of getting the boat—who would drive over and who would sail back—when someone spotted Dallas Truitt beaching the boat.

"I thought I'd sail it on over," Dallas said, "and see about the heroine." He smiled at Quincy.

"I'm fine," she said.

"You were great to tow them in," Melissa said.

"Sure," Dallas said. "Any time."

"Yes, we're very grateful to you," Mrs. Luckie said.

Quincy basked—and got the best piece of steak.

Nineteen

The next day was rainy, and Quincy lay in bed a long time before she got up. She had slept long and hard, and she felt deliciously rested and alive—but not quite ready to get up.

She lay with her arms folded beneath her head and watched the reflections of the water on the sleeping-porch ceiling and thought about the search for the treasure ship. They had worked very hard, and they had failed. Of course, they could keep on looking, but she was afraid they'd never get Molly back in the boat—certainly not out in the Gulf. And she still hesitated to go with Mike alone. That was silly, she thought. But it was better to have three people, wasn't it? Why? Then she remembered that Arthur C. Clarke had said that three people was the optimum number for any dangerous mission. . . .

But to be honest, she thought, I don't want to take that dumb sailboat out in the Gulf again. If only I had a little motorboat, she thought. But it would take a big motorboat to go out into the Gulf. There was no easy solution.

She heard the *plink-plink* of guitars and realized that Jill and Sam were both on the front porch below her. At first she couldn't make out what they were singing. She heard them singing something to the tune of "Yankee Doodle," and they repeated it so much that she finally heard the words:

"Storm Alberta came to shore
A-huffin' and a-puffin' . . .
Took the houses and the docks
And split them like a muffin!"

They were laughing and singing and congratulating themselves.

"That's great, Sam!" Jill said.

"It is good, isn't it?" Sam said.

And they sang it again.

Quincy smiled herself. It was funny. The show was going to be different, all right, this year. Was it all going to be about St. Jerome? She really ought to write a song about LeMoyne. But how? She lay there, trying to get started, but she couldn't think of a thing.

At last she got up and went downstairs and out to the front porch and lay down in the big hammock and listened to Jill and Sam, who were trying to write a chorus to go with their great verse.

Quincy thought again about LeMoyne, the Labrador retriever, and about Petey, Mrs. Standish's little terrier. Dogs. . . . But then her mind idly wandered off to quasars . . . nebulae . . . treasure hunting.

It really is too bad I can't use astronomy to figure out something about the treasure. Could I use the stars and tides or something? Wouldn't that be perfect? Where would I be if I were a Spanish galleon? she wondered to herself.

She floated dreamily in the hammock.

"Oh, you're up?" said Mrs. Luckie, who came out on the porch. "How do you feel this morning?"

"Fine," Quincy said.

"Have you had any breakfast?" Mrs. Luckie asked.

"No, ma'am."

"Come on. I'll fix you some," Mrs. Luckie said.

"*You?*"

"That's right," Mrs. Luckie said. "I *can* cook, you know."

"I can get a bowl of cereal," Quincy said.

"I'll be glad to cook you an egg," Mrs. Luckie said.

"I tell you what," Mr. Luckie said. "I'll make you some pancakes." He had just appeared.

"No, thanks," Quincy said. "I'll go get some cereal." All this attention was wonderful, she thought, but she really did like cereal for breakfast.

She ate her cereal while both her parents sat and watched. That was unnerving. When she'd finished, she started out the front door.

"Where are you going, Ducky?" her mother asked.

"Down to Molly's," Quincy said.

"But it's raining," Mrs. Luckie said.

"I'm not sugar or salt," Quincy said, quoting her grandmother.

"Be back for lunch!" Mr. Luckie said.

"Okay," she said, and she went flying out into the rain and down to the Motts' house. Molly was sitting watching her mother work on another jigsaw puzzle.

Mrs. Mott looked up and said, rather coolly, "Hello, Quincy," and looked back down at her jigsaw puzzle. "You-all had quite an adventure yesterday."

"Yes, ma'am," Quincy said.

"Let's go down to your house," Molly said.

"Okay," Quincy said.

"Let me get an umbrella," Molly said.

Mrs. Mott looked up again and said, "Now, girls, no boating today, okay?"

"Yes, ma'am," Quincy and Molly said together.

"Is she mad?" Quincy asked Molly, as they hurried down the walk to the Luckie house.

"She's glad and she's mad," Molly said. "She's glad I'm not dead, and she's mad because we went sailing out in the Gulf."

"Is she mad at me?" Quincy asked.

"A little, I guess," Molly said. "She'll get over it."

"I hope so," Quincy said.

They were at the Luckies' front porch now, where Sam and Jill were still working away. Molly stopped to listen to them. Quickly they sang their verse to "Yankee Doodle" for her.

> "Storm Alberta came to shore
> A-huffin' and a-puffin'. . . .
> Took the houses and the docks
> And split them like a muffin!"

Molly loved it. She clapped her hands, and her dimples showed. "That's wonderful," she said. Quincy had never seen Molly look so lively.

Jill and Sam did the chorus—as far as they'd gotten—for Molly:

> "Storm Alberta blew it up
> Storm Alberta nasty!
> Tossed the boats around the beach
> And *dah dah dah* be nasty!"

"We can't get a last line," Sam said.

Molly was charmed. "I didn't know that's how you wrote songs," she said. "Oh, I wish I had my guitar—but it's raining and I don't want to go home for it."

"Use Melissa's," Jill said. "Use it. We need all the help we can get if we're going to have enough songs for the Show."

"That's right," said Mrs. Luckie, who was standing around tapping her foot. "The summer's half over. We really have to buckle down."

Molly settled down with Sam and Jill and beamed when Jill praised her and told her she'd learned to play real well.

"We'll have a full orchestra of guitars," Jill said.

"Do a song about LeMoyne," Quincy said. "I keep telling you."

Everybody agreed it was a good idea, but nobody could think of what to say.

"You remember that old Hit Parade song?" Mrs. Luckie said. " 'How Much Is That Doggie in the Window?' "

"Hmmmmm," Jill said.

"What comes next?" Sam said.

"He thinks he's a porpoise, too," sang Mrs. Luckie.

Jill and Molly plonked enthusiastically.

"That's better than that 'Careless Love' thing," Quincy said. "Lots."

"Of course, it doesn't have to be a song about a dog that you use the tune of," Jill said.

"I know," Mrs. Luckie said, but sometimes it just seems to make it easier to think of something . . . association or something."

They were all singing "What's wrong with that doggie in the water?" and Quincy realized that she had lost Molly, at least temporarily. Molly was hooked. She was going to work on the Summer Show, and, furthermore, she was obviously going to enjoy it. Quincy sighed.

Her father came out on the porch with cups of coffee for himself and Mrs. Luckie. "How's it coming?" he asked.

"I think we've got another song," Jill said, and she did the first two lines of "Doggie" again. Then they all burst into "Storm Alberta" for his benefit. All but Quincy.

"Well, you're doing well with the songs," Mr. Luckie said. "But I'd hate to see it become a stand-up revue. We need some action, a story line, or even skits."

"They do revues on Broadway," Mrs. Luckie said. "And remember the Jacques Brel thing at the Alley in Houston."

"That doesn't make it true theater," Mr. Luckie said.

"But for a summer show?" Mrs. Luckie persisted.

At that moment, Mike Standish appeared at the screen door, a newspaper over his head and a paper bag in his hand.

Everyone greeted Mike and asked him how he felt after his adventure, and Mike said he felt fine. He stood around looking ill at ease until the others returned to their music.

Mike began to mouth something at Quincy, and she couldn't understand him. His lips were moving frantically and he was rolling his eyes, but she had no idea what he was trying to say.

"Come in here," she said, and led him into the living room.

"Did you tell them about the treasure?" he asked.

"Yes, I finally did," Quincy said.

"I had to tell my grandparents, too," Mike said. "I just wanted to let you know I had to do it."

"Oh, it's okay," Quincy said. "Nobody cares anyway. What did the Standishes say?"

"You're right," Mike said. "They weren't awfully interested."

"I think my folks have forgotten all about it," Quincy said.

"Well, anyway, I ordered this from a bookstore in New York," Mike said, "and it came yesterday." He pulled a book out of his paper sack. "It's by Jacques Cousteau and it's about diving for sunken treasure."

"Is there anything useful in it?" Quincy asked.

"Well, it's interesting," Mike said.

"Oh, you like it because it's by Cousteau," Quincy said. "I bet you think if *he* did it then it's super."

"I've been willing to look for treasure ships from the beginning," Mike said. "After I recovered from my initial skepticism, I thought it would be good to have a try. . . ."

"What's this? What's this?" asked Mr. Luckie on his way back to the kitchen.

Quincy decided she might very well very soon get tired of her family paying attention to her.

"It's a book on treasure," she said.

"Let me see," Mr. Luckie said, sitting down and flipping through it.

"Let me get the one I got from the library," Quincy said. "It's about the Florida east coast." She ran upstairs and got her book.

Mr. Luckie looked at it, too, and seemed rather interested. "I don't blame you kids for trying to find it," he said.

Mr. Luckie took both books out on the front porch and began showing pictures to Jill and Sam and Mrs. Luckie. Quincy was never sure exactly how it happened, but very soon everyone was looking at the books and talking about treasure diving and everybody decided—before she knew what was happening—that Treasure would be the theme for the Summer Show.

"It has all sorts of possibilities," Jill said. "We can have the Spaniards on the galleon in a storm. . . ."

"We can have the prow of a galleon on stage," Sam said.

"If we could tie their storm to our storm . . . Alberta and the old Spanish storm. . . ."

"Could we have an opening like *The Tempest?*"

They all chattered . . . someone suggested a song, "Storm over the Harbor" to the tune of "Moon over Miami. . . ."

"We could have the galleon sinking. . . ."

"Then we could have centuries go by . . . and St. Jerome becomes a summer colony. . . ."

"And then we could have our storm . . . and use the same music for both storms, maybe?"

"Then we could have the treasure hunters . . . the Intrepid Three."

"And we could do Ducky's heroic swim. . . ."

" 'She fam and she fam right over the dam. . . .' You know, like 'Free Little Fiddies' or whatever that crazy song was. . . ."

"And we could find the treasure!"

"No, leave it hanging. . . . 'Somewhere, under the waters . . .' like 'Somewhere, over the rainbow. . . .' "

"It's going to be great!"

"We've got to get something down on paper. . . ."

"Who's going to be who? When can we start casting?"

"Could Ducky and Molly and Mike play themselves?"

Quincy had listened to all this, and she had to admit she thought it sounded neat and she thought it was stupendous that she and Molly and Mike would be portrayed in the

Show, but she did not want to be in it and have her mother, the director, shouting instructions at her. She just didn't want to be in it.

"I just don't want to do it," she said.

"All right," her mother said, surprising her. It was all part of the new Be-nice-to-Ducky atmosphere, but no matter what the reason, she hoped they kept on being nice to her, but still sort of let her alone once in a while. A happy medium would be nice.

Mike, surprisingly, was quite willing to be in the Show, but everyone agreed now that it would be funnier if other people acted the parts of Molly, Mike, and Quincy. He would be assigned another part, they told him.

Molly plonked away. She did not seem to want to stop.

Twenty

Rehearsals began in earnest for the Summer Show. The Luckies recruited a cast of thousands—the Caldwell children, the Dukes, and all the families from down at the end of the bluff were enlisted.

Rehearsals went on every afternoon and every night in the pavilion.

Quincy stayed away from the pavilion. She spent long hours in the hammock, rereading all her Arthur C. Clarkes and poring over the books on treasure hunting.

She occasionally visited Miss Hattie Hawk, who wasn't in the Show either. Miss Hattie Hawk hadn't gotten around to researching the microfilms of Spanish archives yet. "I won't have time until fall," she said. "I have too much to do down here."

Quincy told Miss Hattie Hawk all about the search they'd conducted, and Miss Hattie Hawk nodded with approval. "I remember that man who found the wreck on the inner tube—off Ft. Pierce, I think it was," she said. "Well, don't give up. Maybe you'll find it yet. And as soon as you do, register it with the state of Florida, and then nobody but you can explore it. Of course, the state gets one fourth of any treasure you salvage."

Miss Hattie Hawk was a gold mine of information, Quincy decided, and the mere fact that she didn't think they were crazy, or dumb kids to look, was encouraging.

But that was all that was encouraging. Quincy had lost her helpers, her team. Molly loved doing music for the Summer Show, and Mike was so happy to be included in a group activity he would do any chore assigned to him. He had several small parts in the Show, and, like Molly, he was busy all the time.

Dallas began working on the lights and recruited Quincy to help with both lighting and sound effects. They improvised wildly. They used aluminum pie plates for reflectors and coffee cans for spotlights. They borrowed anything they could find to make colored lights—even Mrs. Ballew's amber carnival-glass punch bowl.

They taped sounds—the whir of the electric blender, the crackle of newspaper, and Quincy whistling through her teeth—to get something that resembled a storm at sea.

They strung miles of electric wire around the pavilion, and Quincy learned how to splice wires and make electrical connections. That was fun, but Dallas was only there at night, and during the day she was left pretty much on her own.

Except that during the day, her father hung around her, apparently to make sure she was all right. He smiled fondly at her, tousled her hair, and offered to cook pancakes for her.

"What do you want to do on your birthday?" he asked her one day.

147

Quincy had spent every birthday of her life at St. Jerome, and sometimes she felt disadvantaged because she had never had a birthday party in Houston where her school friends could come.

"I don't know," she said.

"Would you like a picnic at Rat Island?" he asked.

"Not really," she said.

"What *would* you like to do?"

"I'd like to go into Azalea and eat at a big restaurant," she said.

Everybody agreed that this was another way Ducky was crazy—she preferred a restaurant to a picnic on Rat Island—but they all went along with her idea. It was, after all, her own birthday, and all Luckies got to spend their birthdays the way they wanted to. It was a tradition of long standing. "Although you do make it hard, Ducky," said Melissa. "Who wants to drive into Azalea and back?"

"It's not *your* birthday," Quincy said. "And I want to ask Dallas to come with us. Is that all right?" she asked her mother.

"It's all right with me, but what about Melissa? He's her friend," said Mrs. Luckie.

Melissa tossed her long black hair back over her shoulders and said she didn't care. "I'm going to break up with him anyway. He's such a hick."

"He is *not*," Quincy said.

"You'll be meeting so many new people when you go East to school," Mrs. Luckie said.

"More of those sissies you like," Quincy said.

"Dallas can come if you want him," Mrs. Luckie said to Quincy.

Meanwhile, Quincy continued to think about the treasure

148

ship she was sure was out there somewhere. As the song for the Show went, "Somewhere, under the waters. . . ."

She found a book on the bookshelf in the living room about sailing techniques, and she read that. She read about tides and currents in the encyclopedia.

One day Mr. Bite came with a crew and began to build a new dock. Quincy sat and watched the men work and gazed beyond them to the tip of Turtle Point. Somewhere out there, in the harbor or the Gulf, was a ship. Where was it?

Suppose there had been a bad storm four hundred years ago and the ship had been looking for a safe harbor—suppose the ship had tried to come into Turtle Harbor.

Tried to come into Turtle Harbor. Suppose the tide was wrong, and the storm was getting worse. How could the tide be wrong? Turtle Harbor wasn't very deep. But it did have the channel down the middle. But what if the ship went aground on the sandbars or the spits? It wouldn't sink because of that, would it? Did a ship have to hit coral or something hard like that to split open and sink? Just running aground on sand wouldn't sink a ship.

What if it was coming in at low tide and that rip current at the tip of Turtle Point slammed it into a sandbar, what would happen? If it were very low tide and the tide was just turning and just beginning to come in, then the current at the Point would be very, very swift and it might smash a galleon into the sandbar at the mouth of the harbor. And if there was a storm, it would batter the ship to pieces.

Wait a minute. Quincy got up off the beach and ran up the steps and inside her house to the living room where, hanging on the wall, was the nautical chart of Turtle Harbor. There was deep water in the small channel where the swift current poured around the tip . . . and there, opposite the tip, was a sandbar.

The ideal conditions, she thought, for a shipwreck. A swift channel at the mouth of a bay—and a sandbar.

She couldn't stand still. She jumped up and down, there, all by herself, in the living room. Then she was able to stand quite still, eyes closed. She was sure she knew where the ship must be. They hadn't looked there at all. They had looked all over the inside of the harbor and then they'd gone right past that place—concerned only with the current next to the tip of Turtle Point—to the Gulf.

When rehearsals broke up in the late afternoon, everybody came down to go in swimming, and Quincy took Mike and Molly aside and told them what she'd figured out.

"It's there," she said. "I know it."

"Maybe you're right," Mike said.

"Let's go look," Quincy said.

"Not me," Molly said.

"In the sailboat?" Mike asked. He looked very doubtful.

"Not in any boat," Molly said.

"Come on," Quincy said. "Just over to the tip of Turtle Point and that little channel. On a sunny day, I bet we can see to the bottom without any trouble. Come on."

"Not me," Molly said.

"I don't know," Mike said. "That channel was kind of scary the day we went out to the Gulf. I'm awful busy, besides—with the Show."

He sounded just like Jill and the others, Quincy thought. It was disgusting.

Twenty-one

Quincy simmered. She was sure she knew where the wreck was, but she had no crew, no mask, no float. And she had no courage, she told herself. She was defeated, she decided.

For a few days, she even gave up reading and sat in the pavilion watching rehearsals. She found herself trying to write a song for the Show. I'll end up like everybody else, she said to herself.

But then her birthday came, and she got up early and went downstairs. Her presents were piled on the kitchen table—there was a new mask and snorkel, some flippers, a new float. And there was money, to "buy books with."

"We couldn't be sure which Arthur C. Clarkes you owned and which ones you'd read and all that," her mother said.

Her father made her some French toast for breakfast, and everybody wished her a happy birthday and even said it was great they were going into Azalea that night for her birthday dinner.

And then everybody disappeared to the pavilion. The

big project for the day was painting the Spanish galleon Melissa had designed for the first-act set.

Quincy offered to help paint, but her mother said she didn't have to since it was her birthday. She wandered out on the front porch and looked at Turtle Point. The tip stuck out into the water in a little white curve, and she thought she could see the ripples of the current in the narrow channel that whipped around the tip. Right there, she thought, that's where it is. She knew it.

Why not go ahead and look? She had a mask and a float again. She wouldn't be going out in the Gulf, not really, but just over to Turtle Point. She could "check out" by leaving a note on the refrigerator door. She wrote the note—"Am out in boat by Turtle Point"—and fastened it to the refrigerator with cellophane tape. She gathered up a paddle, a ski belt, float, mask, snorkel, and flippers and went down to the beach and dumped them into the sailboat. She pulled the boat out into the water and got in and turned it around to catch the wind and set out across Turtle Harbor.

She had never been in a boat by herself before. She felt a little like an astronaut, she thought, one of the early ones who went into space alone, like John Glenn or Alan Shepard. She thought about the man who sailed *Tinker-belle*, a boat not much bigger than this one, across the Atlantic alone. Would she like to do that? Not at all, she thought. She'd rather go into space.

It was easy to skim across the sparkling water of Turtle Harbor that morning to the tip of the Point, and it was simple to bring the boat about into the wind and beach it. She put on her ski belt and flippers and mask and set out with the float.

As soon as she got in the water, away from the boat, the

current in the channel carried her rapidly around the tip of the Point into the bay waters. The ride was fun. She wished she weren't all alone. Someday they'd have to come over, everybody, and ride floats and inner tubes around the Point in this channel. But that wasn't what she'd come for today.

She tried paddling the float across the current, and she couldn't get anywhere because the current was too strong. She pulled herself up on the beach at the harbor side and considered the situation.

Could she swim out on the Gulf side, go past the current, and come toward the harbor on the far side of the current?

She tried it and found it was a long swim out past the swiftest part of the current, and the water tended always to swing her back into the deepest, fastest part of the channel.

But when she finally got far enough out, although it was hard to stay in one place, she could put her head down and look. She was sure she could see dark masses on the bottom.

What were they? Seaweed? It was hard to tell. The current moved her inexorably over into the harbor, and she swam back to the tip of Turtle Point and walked across it to the Gulf side and swam far out again and around the channel to have another look. This time, she thought she saw the masses again—on the bottom of the little channel near the sandbar.

She repeated her maneuver—drifting with the current to the harbor, swimming to the Point, walking to the Gulf, swimming out and around, and drifting to have another look. It was hot work. She lost count of the times she did it, but gradually she became sure that she was seeing something large and dark and alien on the bottom. It was hard to decide what the masses were because the water shifted continually, and the light and shadows changing on the bottom made it hard to identify anything.

But at last she was sure there was a pile of ballast rock near the foot of the reef. She decided she might be able to do better without the float, now that she knew where to look. She swam out into the Gulf, turned back past the channel, and treaded water until she had her bearings. Then she began to look down. There it was. She dived as deep as she could. There was no mistake. There was a huge pile of junk on the bottom—too deep to be dangerous to the small pleasure boats that passed on their way in and out of Turtle Harbor.

She swam back to the Point, got the sailboat, took it out and anchored it on the sandbar, and slipped overboard to have another look. It was still there. She climbed back into the boat and noted its position in relation to two points on land—and then set out for home, feeling like a conquering hero.

She found herself humming, and the words to a song leaped to her mind, and they easily fit the tune of "My Country, 'Tis of Thee," and she began to sing them as she sailed.

> "My treasure is right here,
> Bright gold and silver clear!
> I know it is!"

She belted it out, an anthem of joy, and the boat seemed to fly across Turtle Harbor to St. Jerome.

Twenty-two

She went through the house and took her note off the refrigerator door and then went out to the pavilion.

"I found it!" she said. "I found it!"

The painters all looked up and stared at her.

"I found the treasure," she said. "I know I did."

At first nobody but Mike and Molly knew exactly what she was talking about. The others regarded treasure as something fictional, to write a show about. But everybody listened while she explained how she'd figured out where the ship had to have gone down and how her theory was almost bound to be proved by what she'd seen over near the tip of Turtle Point.

"Let's all go see," Mrs. Luckie said. "We can take the sailboat and Grandpapa's boat. . . ."

To Quincy's amazement, everybody stopped work on the sets and went and put on bathing suits and collared Mr. Ballew and got him to bring his boat along, and everybody who could get into the two boats came along.

"It's so easy once you know where to look," Quincy said.

Everybody but Molly Mott went into the water to dive

down and look at what they were sure was ballast rock, and everyone applauded Quincy's cleverness.

"Will we all be rich?" Molly Mott asked.

"I don't care," Quincy said. "It's just that we found it. It's the idea that I found a Spanish galleon!"

"If that's what it is," Jill said.

"That could be something else," Sam said.

"I bet it's the wreck," Mike said.

When they were all back at St. Jerome and dry again, reaction set in.

"You took the boat out without checking out," Mr. Luckie said.

"I left a note on the refrigerator door," Quincy said. "Everybody was busy. And I wanted to look right then. I had to look."

"It is very unscientific to go out alone without telling us," Mr. Luckie said, but he wasn't screaming. Everybody knew that kids had been taking boats out alone at St. Jerome for forty years and that "checking out" had not been formally observed.

"But it's a good rule," Mrs. Luckie said.

"Anyway, I wrote a song," Quincy said.

"You wrote a song?" said Jill. "Let's hear it."

And Quincy sang, as best she could, her song to the tune of "My Country, 'Tis of Thee."

> "My treasure is right here,
> Bright gold and silver clear
> I know it is!"

They loved it. Everybody agreed it could be the Summer Show's grand finale. And it could replace "Somewhere Under the Waters," which nobody had liked much.

"The whole cast can join in," Jill said.

"Let the audience join in, too," Mrs. Luckie said, "since the tune's so simple. We can print the words on a big board and everybody can sing."

"But what do we do about the treasure?" Quincy asked.

How did you actually salvage a ship? What should they do? Everybody had read newspaper accounts but nobody had anything more than the vaguest idea of how you went about it.

Quincy and Mike knew the most since they'd read the books.

"You have to hire a salvage crew," Quincy said, "with deep-sea divers."

"Jacques Cousteau had big boats and launches and radar and an air compressor and airlifts," Mike said. "The airlift brought stuff up from the bottom and dumped it into metal baskets. Then the crew sifted it."

"The Real Eight Company used a homemade dredge and a team of underwater divers to go through the ballast rock," Quincy said.

Dredges and air compressors—it sounded frightfully complicated and expensive, everyone agreed.

"You have to register the wreck with the state of Florida," Quincy said. "Miss Hattie Hawk told me that."

Then everyone agreed that the first thing to do was get a diver to go down and make sure the pile of stuff really was a wreck—and an old wreck, one worth salvaging.

At that point Dallas Truitt arrived for Quincy's birthday trip to Azalea.

"Let Dallas do it!" Quincy said. "He knows everything about the sea!"

"Thanks," Dallas said.

"Have you ever done any diving?" Mr. Luckie asked him.

157

"A little," Dallas said.

Dallas finally found out what they were talking about and said he and Buddy could go down and do a little preliminary exploring. "We'll do it tomorrow," he said.

"What if somebody beats us to it?" Quincy said.

"It can wait one day," Mr. Luckie said.

After dinner in the steakhouse in Azalea that night, Mr. Luckie banged on the table for attention. "I have an announcement to make," he said. "This may be Ducky's real birthday present. Sarah and I have decided that Ducky's right—we shouldn't spend all of every summer at the beach. We won't come to St. Jerome for the whole summer next year. Ducky, you can go to Rice's summer school, and we'll come when that's over—the middle of July."

A groan went up from Jill and Sam and Melissa.

"I was just beginning to like it here," Quincy said.

"Are you serious?" Mr. Luckie said.

"No. I mean, I'd *love* to go to Rice's summer school—you know that. I mean, it has been fun finding treasure and all. That's all I meant."

"Besides, I need to be where there's a library myself for part of the summer," Mr. Luckie said.

"I can at least get a better job in Houston than in that dumb Shell Shop," Melissa said. "But then I'd have to work all summer there—you mean I wouldn't get to come to St. Jerome at all?"

"All those details can be worked out," Mr. Luckie said.

"We're making a commitment to Quincy," Mrs. Luckie said. "If she wants to take astronomy or whatever it is, she can."

Quincy felt grateful to her mother on two counts . . . Mrs. Luckie was the one who loved St. Jerome the most, and she had called her Quincy instead of Ducky.

158

"You know, it might be fun to spend part of a summer somewhere else," Jill said. "The Rockies? Cape Cod?"

"Paris?" Mrs. Luckie said.

"Houston," Mr. Luckie said. "Don't get grandiose ideas."

"But we'll be rich from the treasure," Melissa said.

The next day, while Quincy and Mike and Molly watched from the tip of Turtle Point, Buddy and Dallas took turns diving to the bottom of the reef. They confirmed it was a wreck. They saw a cannon, thickly encrusted with barnacles and corrosion, and a huge anchor near the ballast rock.

The Summer Show was abandoned for three whole days while everybody tried to decide what to do.

Miss Hattie Hawk was consulted.

"Get in touch with the state," she said.

Mr. Luckie drove to Elysium to use the pay phone outside the Shell Shop. With Dallas and Quincy standing beside him, he called the state offices in Tallahassee to find out about salvage permits.

They sought advice from the only lawyer in Elysium—they found him fishing off the dock of the *Queen of Elysium*, the party fishing boat that went out in the Gulf every day—about forming a salvage corporation.

The only thing was that when it got right down to it, nobody wanted to fool with a salvage company, except Dallas Truitt, and, oddly, Miss Hattie Hawk.

"I've got four children to educate," complained Mr. Luckie. "I can't put any money into salvage."

"Well, I'll do it," Miss Hattie Hawk said. "I'd just as soon invest my life savings in a salvage corporation as in a company that makes napalm," said Miss Hattie Hawk. "Or aerosol cans." She agreed to finance a small treasure expedition, hire Dallas to run the operation, and cut Quincy, Mike, and Molly in for a small share of any profits.

Quincy went with Miss Hattie Hawk and Dallas and her father to the state offices in Tallahassee to apply for the salvage permit. They filled out forms in triplicate, and the air-conditioned offices seemed a long way from doubloons and onion-shaped wine bottles. But the secretaries behind the counter all smiled at them and wished them luck and told them about the odd characters who came in to apply for permits.

"It's all so educational," Mrs. Luckie said when they got back.

"It's all exhausting," Mr. Luckie said. "It's worse than the dock committee."

But at last the papers were signed, and it was all up to Dallas and Miss Hattie Hawk.

Back to the Summer Show.

Twenty-three

And the Summer Show was a big success, too.

"The best ever," everyone agreed.

The Show began with the arrival of the Narváez expedition, accompanied by the clanking of garbage-can-lid armor. The Spaniards made camp, singing to the tune of "Oh Careless Love," the words:

> "St. Jerome, oh, St. Jerome . . .
> Here we are at last!"

A galleon sailed on stage—the great painted cardboard galleon designed by Melissa—and was "wrecked" in a magnificent storm, with sound effects devised by Dallas and Quincy.

The Narváez men waited to be picked up by the galleon—which had disappeared in the storm—and when it never came, tried to build boats and finally took off to sea.

There came another great storm, which wrecked their little boats. More sound and light by Dallas and Quincy.

Time passed, and the summer colonists arrived. When the

contemporary part began, the audience began to make audible comments and to join in.

Melissa was Miss Hattie Hawk, striding across the beach identifying birds, shells, weeds, and fish in pig latin.

Other young people acted the parts of Mrs. Ballew knitting, Mrs. Standish shelling peas, Mrs. Luckie doing needlepoint, Mr. Ballew with pipe and floppy hat pulling his shark line.

The "Doggie" number immortalized LeMoyne and Petey.

Then came the storm Alberta, with more lights and ominous sounds. And the dock committee meetings began.

Three very small children acted the parts of Quincy, Molly, and Mike, who found coins on the beach. To the tune of "Sugar in the Morning," they lisped the ditty about "Treasure in the mornin', treasure in the evenin' . . . ," which stopped the show.

Then Quincy and Molly and Mike were caught in the fourth storm of the show—more lights and sounds—and the boat capsized. The chorus sang Jill's song about Quincy, "She fam and she fam. . . ."

The dock was rebuilt, and the chorus sang "Our Dock Is New."

At the very last, Jill played the part of Quincy and sang "My Treasure Is Right Here," and the whole cast came onstage and sang it. Then the audience joined in.

"Do it over!" shouted the audience when the music stopped. Most of the audience had been in the Show or helped backstage, but everybody wanted to hear the songs over, so the cast obliged. The sound effects were replayed, too, to much applause.

Mr. Luckie brought out three freezers of ice cream he'd made for the occasion, and everyone gasped.

162

"We'll never see the like of this again," Grandmama said.

Quincy felt good. The Show was over, and she'd helped. She'd written a song, and she'd learned a lot about electricity. And the Show had been fun. She had to admit it. And she would have felt awful if she hadn't done anything to help, if she hadn't been a part of it in some way. Things like the Show were really kind of exciting. When they were all over, everybody felt good, as though it were Christmas. It brought everybody together, or something. It was probably even worth all the time and effort people put into it, Quincy decided.

"That wasn't so bad, was it?" she said to Molly.

"It was great," Molly said. "Guess what, Quincy. Mike Standish is going to stay in Azalea and go to school this winter. He's going to live with his grandparents."

Quincy was startled. "Is he pleased?"

"He says it's a good thing. He says he'll miss the Museum of Natural whatever-it-is, but that he'll be closer to the woods and the coast for finding creatures," Molly said.

"I wonder how he'll fit in at Azalea High School," Quincy said.

"I think he'll fit in just fine," Molly Mott said, with unexpected firmness. "He's sure to win first place in the Science Fair, for one thing." She paused. "And he's going to help me with my entry."

"Your entry?" Quincy was startled again. "You mean you're going to enter the Science Fair?"

"Mike is going to help me with my demonstration . . . it's going to be on bleaching hairs. Do you think Melissa would give me some of her black hair?"

Quincy felt that bleaching hair wasn't science—it was

home economics. But then, there were all kinds of science. Molly was smiling, as she ate ice cream. "I think that's great," Quincy said to her. "I bet you and Mike have a wonderful time at Azalea High! You'll make it famous."

"It won't be so bad," Molly said. "It's going to cheer my Mom up to have me enter the Science Fair."

Quincy wandered off, and decided she'd have to digest all this about Molly and Mike and went outside and through the yards and to the steps in front of the Luckie house . . . and down to the beach. She looked at the sky, spotted Polaris, and walked out on the dock. The nice new dock.

She heard somebody behind her and turned and saw that it was Dallas.

"Listen, Quincy," Dallas said, "I just want to say to you in case I don't have a chance before you leave, keep on keeping on."

"Keep on keeping on?" she asked.

"Keep on with science," Dallas said. "You're a great girl. Your family's great, but you're the smartest one in it, and don't forget it. You're different from them, and it's not going to be easy, but you can win in the end. People that can do science can do anything.

"Really?" Quincy said. She was almost whispering. It was like a daydream, to have Dallas saying things like this to her. "Keeping on doing what?"

"Keeping on reading. Keep on looking in the telescope. Keep on studying. Learn to use a computer. Take all the math and science you can get. Keep on after your family to let you do your own thing. Don't get discouraged."

"I won't," Quincy said, and she was happy that her voice sounded a little stronger.

"You're a star," Dallas said. "It may not be easy—but

your family will understand someday maybe. And anyway, everybody has some family handicap to overcome."

"I know," Quincy said, "like Mike and Molly and their parents."

"And me and my family."

Dallas leaned over and kissed her on the cheek and took her hand and squeezed it.

Quincy didn't know what to say. She loved what he'd said to her—who wouldn't? But what to say to him?

"Thanks," she said. "Thanks for letting me talk to you this summer. And thanks for towing us in."

Maybe I will be glad to be grown up, she thought. Then I'll know better what to say.

They walked off the dock together and across the beach, with moonlight falling all around them. Quincy looked up at the moon—my moon, she thought—and walked along beside Dallas. She didn't have to say anything else, she thought.

They went up the steps and back to the pavilion.

"Where *have* you been?" Melissa said, as they came back inside.

"Stargazing," said Dallas. "Looking at a star."

Epilogue

It turned out to be a very small treasure ship.

Nobody got rich. Dallas made enough to finish school on.

Miss Hattie Hawk gave nearly everything they salvaged to the state museum.

Quincy's share turned out to be what she thought was the best thing that came up from the bottom. Dallas mailed it to her in time for Christmas. It was an astrolabe, an ancient navigating instrument which Spanish sailors had used to take sights at sea of heavenly bodies.

But people still find doubloons on the beaches of Turtle Harbor after a storm.